DATE DUE

LONG LIVE THE SUICIDE KING

AARON MICHAEL RITCHEY

courtney**literary**

Courtney Literary, LLC, Colorado Springs
www.courtneyliterary.com

This Book Dedication Spans Verb Tenses:

In the past tense,
this one is for my GROUP of high school friends.
Thanks, Ryan, for bringing us all together in your yellow house.

In the present tense,
this one is for the Evergreen Critique Group,
for Jan Gurney and Diane Dodge and our Monday nights.

In the future tense,
this is another one for all of those living on just this side of hopeless:
the saints, the sinners, the gangsters and the geeks.

LONG LIVE THE SUICIDE KING

CHAPTER ONE

WHERE THE FUN STOPS HERE

Three days free of the THC and I'm feeling every minute of it. Out of my last class, I'm sweating like a fat guy telling jokes. Not that I'm some sweaty, trainspotting type of heroin addict. Not even. I just needed some clean time.

It's a Wednesday escape from Coyote Ridge High School. People are hustling across the student parking lot to their cars and I have my head down, backpack on my shoulder, hell bent on getting home.

Up walks the new girl with her black leather jacket open like wings. She is blonde and smiling. Too nice a combination. The pink of her lipstick pushes me to the edge.

"Hey JD," she says. "Do you want to walk to the bridge with me?"

I open and close my mouth like a speared carp. Her name. What's her name? I don't have time for this. I have to get home before I find myself at the bridge.

"Where have you been the last couple of days?" the new girl asks. Can't tell her the truth. Not yet.

"I've had school stuff," I say, which she'll probably believe, because I'm the only one in our little bridge crew who does homework.

"You're in all those AP classes, huh?" she asks.

"Yeah," I say and my brain is trying to pull me away, but my heart just wants to go with her to smoke blunts and Camels with my old friends, but really I'm spending most of my time trying to keep my eyes off the luscious plunge of her shirt and all that pale, white skin.

I can smell the wonderful mix of perfume, cigarettes and leather surrounding her.

I know I'm going to go with her. I have to go with her. Please, God, let me go with her.

But I know what that will lead to.

Gotta get home. Now, more than ever. Gotta get home. Gotta get home. Gotta get home. My mantra, my salvation, the three words my life has become.

"Gotta get home," I say dutifully. I see her face drop. She likes me. Why this day? Only three days clean. Painfully clean. So clean I feel dirty.

I try to salvage something with the girl. "Sorry, just a bad day."

"No problem, I understand." She doesn't.

We walk past the portable classrooms and across the football field and stop. To the right is the way to the bridge and my chemical romance. To the left lies the way home.

"Sure I can't tempt you?" she says, all flirty.

"Too late for that." I raise my hand. "Tempted."

"So?"

I smile, throw her a wave, and creep away in my insanity.

Off I go across the field, down the sidewalk, past houses, through traffic lights, speeding home through the one mile of Colorado suburban jungle. I know once I get home, I'll be relatively safe in the luxurious house my parents work themselves into the grave to afford.

Funny, I get past the girl but stop at the dog.

It's the dog that kills me. Every day I walk by that dog, and every day the little rat terrier barks at me. Not that I know what kind of dog it is. The name fits, though. More rat than terrier for sure.

I don't quite know what happens. I mean, the idea must've been slithering around under my skin like a body snatching alien for a while. Watching my grandpa go like he did. Watching my parents dig trenches in their marriage. How long can a Gallipoli marriage last, anyway? And then six months ago there was my ex, Sylvia Dickenson, and her let's-go-back-to-being-friends way of shredding my soul into long strips, perfect for paper mache. Sure, life stuff. Normal and dumb.

But before it all, the idea was there. What kicks it solidly into my head is that yappy little white dog.

The dog starts up his maniacal barking like I'm going to jump the fence and steal his kibbles and bits and bits and bits. I stop, though I know I gotta get home, and suddenly, I hate this pathetic dog snarling at me like it's a two hundred pound Rottweiler.

I yell at the stupid thing. "Dog, what's your deal? Don't you know what you are?"

I bet I'm the only guy to ever just stop and talk to it, and it goes crazy. The bark morphs into this guttural cough, like it swallowed a chainsaw and was trying to spit it out.

"Dog, you have got to get a grip on reality. I could kick you into tomorrow."

It starts running up and down the fence line, and all it wants in the world is to leap over the fence and open up my carotid artery and cry victory.

Yeah, life is real fair. The one day I mess with the dog, the owner is home, unbathed, and half-drunk. Maybe all the way drunk, who knows? He storms out of the house, wife-beater on his chest, eight o'clock shadow on his face, and construction worker muscles on tattooed arms.

I should have lowered my head and fled. But I didn't. Only God knows why. If there is a God.

"What the hell you doin' to my dog?" he yells at me.

I'm not a loud mouth. I mean, I am, but only with my friends, where I can relax. Among the great unwashed, I don't like to talk. I usually get all nervous and my voice gets rubber-band weak.

But that day, with the dog coughing up razor blades, I lose it. My care button breaks.

I say these words in a voice reinforced with iron rebar. "You have a kick-dog. I was going to kick it."

If the construction worker guy had been a dog, he would have started that same snarl.

"You just try it, you little…and I'll kill you."

Cha-ching! Those are the right words. The secret combination that makes me open my mouth, and I say exactly what I have been feeling all along, maybe my whole life. "Good. Do it. Kill me."

I'm shaking, but inside I'm strangely calm.

"What did you say?" the construction worker asks, his face twisted in complete, monstrous disbelief.

I even nod, when I say, "Yeah, kill me, man. Kill me for hating your stupid dog. Put me out of all our misery."

"Leave my dog alone," he says, and I see it. He's not going to kill me. He's a coward. I kick his fence.

It's the rattling ring of the chain-link fence that draws the crowd of kids walking home from school. Everybody loves a fight.

Construction worker guy glances up at all the people, leans over, and spits when he whispers, "Lay off, you little freak."

I feel the eyes of all those good, law-abiding students digging into my back, and I goad the proud dog owner. "Dude, are you going to kill me, or what? You do have a gun, don't you? You look like a guy who adores the Second Amendment."

He's going to bail. I can see it. He and his dog started the suicide, but he's not going to help me finish it. In the end, I'm going to have to do it myself.

"Leave my dog alone," he says and marches off to his house with the dog in his arms. I won. Now, time to get home to give death a booty call.

"I'll kill you," a voice breaks from the crowd. "Come over here, and I'll do it."

It's Brad Sutter. Football player, bully, terrorist, king.

CHAPTER TWO

TAKE A HIT FROM THE JOCK
AND THEN YOU'RE THROUGH

There's Sutter, calling me out. Waiting for me like ye gladiator of olde.

Damn. Good. I drop my backpack onto the sidewalk.

As I walk through the crowd, I bump into Marianne Hartley, and she tries to get in my way. But she means nothing to me, and I mean nothing to her, and so I keep going. It's like I'm floating through the crowd to get to Sutter. My legs are shaking, my stomach is all messed up, and I'm dripping sweat. Yeah, all of that, but inside I'm strangely calm.

Sutter has the glowing blond hair and jocky smirk of a good football player gone bad. His big linebacker body is death on two legs for running backs and cheerleaders alike. Perfect. Let's have this bastard kill me. He'll probably get a medal from the Young Republicans.

6

Sutter has never spoken a word to me in the whole stupid history of our schooling together. Never a single word. But there he stands, my killer and my savior.

"Why do you want to die anyway?" he asks.

"Why do you want to live?"

We square off like boxers. I'm waiting for him to cliché me with the tagline of a boxing movie. Instead he smirks. "I love life, but then I'm not some stoner waste loser like you."

"Yeah, Brad, if I were you, I would totally want to live." I spew beautiful truth. "Let's paint a little picture, shall we? You'll hurt your knee in college, and there goes your football career, and you'll wind up with some nagging, cow-eyed ho who'll pump out some kids, and you'll get fat, and your kids will grow up to be as ignorant and blind as you, and you'll die a broken, pudgy man dreaming about your four years of glory in high school. Yeah, Brad, I want to live for that. Sounds peachy."

He's glaring at me, trying to process all of the multi-syllabic words.

I make it easy for him. "You're just another stupid jock who'll end up nowhere."

His fists curl and uncurl, like a surreal yo-yo with fingers. "You're real smart," he says.

"Are you going to hit me or what?"

He bellies up to me, and we're nose to nose.

I can smell his stink.

"Yeah, Dillenger, and your life is so perfect." He's spitting and I'm catching. Gross.

"My life? That's easy, Brad. Same as you. The exact same as you, but you'll get more action along the way. I'll marry someone I don't really like, have kids I don't really want, work at some horrific job I loathe and die old and all Alzheimered out." First part, just like my dad. Last part, just like my grandfather. I think I said too much.

His eyes glow with hate.

7

"But all that's immaterial, Brad." I say his first name long and hard because no one calls him Brad. "Oh, I'm sorry. Immaterial is probably too big a word for you. Too bad we don't have time for a vocabulary lesson. Are you going to kill me or not?"

I'm right in his face. Kissing close.

"Come on, Sutter, come on. There is only one thing you're good at, and I'm asking you to do it. Do you have the sack to take me out?"

I see his eyes flicker away. He's just like the construction worker. All talk. No murder.

"Punk!" I spit the "p."

He hits me. I go down. In your typical high school fight, we would have wound up on the ground, wrestling around in each other's sweat. The crowd surges forward, expecting us to grapple like refugees from an Ultimate Fighting Championship tournament.

From the ground, I look up at him, blood dribbling over my upper lip, presumably from my nose. Funny, but I scraped my hands on the sidewalk, and they hurt more than my nose.

"Come on, Brad, you can do better than that. I think you're gonna have to strangle me or something."

Sutter seems to ponder my request. Everyone is whispering about this non-fight. This massacre. My public suicide. Great, how many other people in the crowd have I poisoned? Was I going to spread suicidal cheer like some demented Johnny Appleseed?

I hate him. I hate them all, just like I hate the construction worker and his little dog, Toto, too. "Don't just stand there, Brad. I thought you were going to kill me. Come on, moron. Kill me!"

Total Pavlovian response. All doubt is gone. He comes right at me, and suddenly Marianne is there, standing over me, like Joan of Arc before the hordes. Somehow, she forced her way through the crowds. Like with Sutter, I had never talked to nice, sweet, pretty Marianne before my special senior year.

"Leave him alone, Brad," Marianne says. And the way she says it, you know they know each other. How that could be? I have no clue. Different orbits, yet, they know each other.

8

Marianne is calling an end to the fight. It's unprecedented. Nobody stops fights. Nobody. Not even uber-Christian girls like Marianne Hartley.

I stand up. "Brad, I gotta go. I'm thinking hanging might be better than being beaten to death."

"Or sleeping pills!" A kind suggestion comes from the crowd, sympathetic to my suicidal needs.

I try and save face. I hate me sometimes. "But Brad, believe you me, buddy, if I need help with this, you'll be the first person I call."

He says a bunch of stuff, but I grab my backpack and walk off.

I don't thank Marianne or even look at her. I don't see Brad's reaction to her humanitarian efforts. I just walk. I don't know, around her I feel unclean or something.

I head for home. No bridge crew, no new girl, no relapse. Just home.

Annie. That was the new girl's name.

Too late for love. I have to hurry home and figure out the best way to shuffle off this mortal coil. Did I mention I'm in AP English? You gotta love Shakespeare. Now there was a guy who knew something about suicide.

I don't get home right away though. Dumb life. It gets in the way of everything. Including death.

CHAPTER THREE

NEEDS HELP

I cross Rudyard and head up the hill to my not-so-humble abode. Not quite a mansion on a hill, but it's not like my best friend Todd's ghetto house either. I live in what you would call a gated community, a carefully planned sub-metropolitan neighborhood, otherwise known as a house farm. Like the houses were corn, sprouting up from the ground, all close together, all exactly the same.

I toss a nod to the security guard in his little guard room by the gate. He pretends he knows me, but doesn't. And who cares about some kid in black without a car anyway?

My walking problem didn't have to do with an actual lack of automobile, but more of a driver's license issue. All that wouldn't matter in a couple of minutes. The dead don't need to drive.

Up one more hill and around a corner, I see my house and the scrawny little aspens out front. Aspens need water, but where I live, it's dry. All the trees in the neighborhood are small, more like weeds than anything. Lawns gleam green, which is vital among the suburban elite.

I'm walking past the neighbor's house to the south when another dog comes out at me. I know this one. It's Schatzi, a smiley mid-sized dog. His coat is the color of vanilla-bean ice cream. Some million-year-old woman with the unlikely name of Inga Blute owns him. I'd only talked to her a few times. She has short, short hair the color of steel wool. She's German, which makes sense, since she has a roadmap of Munich for a face.

"Hey, Schatzi," I say. "Sorry I can't pet you, but I have to rush on home and kill myself. You understand, I'm sure."

Schatzi barks, casually, like he's trying to bum a cigarette. Or remind me about something from school.

"Schatzi, is someone there?" Mrs. Blute's voice comes out of a row of bushes framing her front porch. In my neighborhood, front porches are like ceremonial daggers—no one uses them, but they look pretty.

Schatzi barks again, as if to answer her. I have a Lassie moment. Billy must have fallen in the well.

"Mrs. Blute, is that you?" I ask. Stupid question because who else would it be?

"Yes, could you help me?"

No, I can't help her. I have to get home and leave behind the world of the living. But then I think I might as well do one last act of kindness. A good legacy to leave behind.

Schatzi follows me up the path wagging his tail. Flowers line the concrete, drooping and fading, since it's fall. A few still have some color, obviously freshly planted. But who plants flowers in the fall? Talk about a complete waste of time.

I find Mrs. Blute wedged between her bushes and her porch. It's a classic I've-fallen-and-I-can't-get-up moment.

I rush into action and pull her upright. She doesn't weigh a thing. Somehow, I connect her body with the dying flowers in her front yard. I imagine they weigh the same. She smells like old woman and the subtle spice of some perfume. She's wearing a cowboy shirt and

11

powder-blue Levi's, faded almost white. She probably bought them a hundred years ago with a chicken and some colored beads.

"Thank you, James. Is that your name?" Her voice is raspy and accented. I expect her to order me around. German is a good language for that.

"Well, sure, Jim, Jimmy, James, JD, whatever."

She leans on me, and I help her to the door. I still have my backpack on, but she's so slight, I'm thinking the backpack is heavier.

"My hip is *nicht so gut*," she says. "I have to get it replaced, but I hate the idea of surgery. I was foolish to go out without my cane, but I felt so strong today."

Wow, she got all German on me. *Nicht so gut* means not so good. I'm a genius.

I hold her as she pushes open the door, and then I guide her into the house. She continues to chatter. "I was just on my way to get the mail. Such a big journey now, to get the mail. What an adventure this life is."

I'm thinking she's being ironic, or sarcastic, or bitter. But I'm not quite sure.

"Yes," I say, "a big huge adventure. Pinch me, I'm dreaming." I don't hide any of my bitter, ironic sarcasm.

Her house is cluttered—not hoarder packed, but lived in full. Lots of bookcases jammed with books. An old musket is over the fireplace. Swords are sprinkled liberally around the room. Framed maps and paintings cover the walls, and the whole place feels far more like a museum than a McMansion. Not like my house. My house is eerily staged with furniture and furnishings, like someone at any minute is going to come in and shoot an instant coffee commercial. Or my parents have been trying to sell it since I was three.

I sit Mrs. Blute down gently in a dining room chair. Well, part dining room chair, part throne, intricately carved. The whole dining room set would look perfectly at home in a medieval castle. Suddenly, I'm curious about Inga Blute, but then, I have to go home and dial up the Grim Reaper.

She eyes me while she rubs at her right hip. "How old are you, James?"

"Seventeen," I say. Seventeen, senior in high school, with about fifteen minutes left to live.

"So young to be feeling such *Weltschmertz*." She has blue eyes that look almost vampiric. Her gaze is so intense, I have to look away.

"*Weltschmertz*?" I ask. "Sorry, I left my German to English dictionary in my other pants."

"Yes, an interesting word. It means the pain of the world, or a world-weariness. Now, what could have you feeling so heavy and sad? You have your whole life ahead of you."

I stifle a burst of laughter. I'm hoping she thinks I belched. "Um, yeah, I have that."

No, I didn't. Had she heard me talking to Schatzi? Or was she psychic?

"When I was your age," she said, "I traveled all over Europe after the war. Germany was not a place I wanted to be anymore. Bad memories, but you don't want to hear about that. Old people and their stories bore you, I'm sure."

When someone says something like that, you're supposed to be polite, protest, and say, "No, no, I would love to hear all about the minutia of your life." I'm too busy itching to get on with my dying to be polite.

When I don't say anything, she laughs. Not a chuckle, but a big ol' belly laugh. "Thank you, James. I won't keep you from your very important business. Thank you for rescuing me."

I shrug. "Sure. Anytime. Are you going to be okay?"

"Are you?"

Such the poignant question. Easy answer. "Oh yeah. Me? I'm just fine."

I turn to leave. Schatzi is looking up at me, tongue out, tail swinging, the happiest creature in the universe.

The door is open and I can see the flowers again. Before I know it, I go back to her. "Mrs. Blute—"

She cuts me off. "Inga, please. I will always be Inga. Ingalora, in my schoolgirl days, but now just Inga."

"Inga, you weren't kidding when you said getting the mail was an adventure. Do you really believe that?"

She smiles. Warmly. "Oh, James, I don't have much time left. It's all an adventure to me now."

"What keeps you going?" I ask. It's a question I would be asking a lot in the coming weeks.

"My heart is filled with *joie de vivre*, as the French would say. You don't have it now, but you will. Once you can see the end, once you can measure out your heartbeats in teaspoons, every moment becomes precious. You are young. You think you will live forever, but even now, the clock ticks, James. Tick, tock, tick, tock."

I totally get the cliché she's dishing out, and so it's easy to smile. "Yeah, time waits for no man. Sure. Glad I could help, Inga. I gotta go."

Time to punch my own clock and not give God the satisfaction.

"Come back and visit me, James. I promise I won't talk, only listen. I want to hear more about your adventures and your *Weltschmertz*."

"Sure." Lie.

Inga Blute might have a lust for life, but I don't want life anymore. I don't want to roll the dice to see if I became some cool old person like her, questing for mail, planting flowers in the autumn. Most likely, I'd roll snake-eyes and end up like my grandfather, weeping over a stupid life while dying a stupid death.

I'm not going to take that gamble. I'm going to cash in my chips and leave Las Vegas forever.

CHAPTER FOUR

OF A WHACKED-OUT CHILDREN'S BOOK

I close Inga's front door behind me but lock it before I do.

Anger floods me. How pathetic. She lives this amazing life, or so it would seem from the relics in her house, and then she gets so old getting the mail is this big adventure. It's not fair. This whole set up, life, aging, death, it's all so much bullshit.

I walk down the path, and for fun, kick a dying flower out of the soil. It doesn't matter. In a few weeks, either Inga or her gardener will be tearing them all out anyway.

Back in my own eerily staged house, I notice the smell right away. Inga's house smells like coffee, books, and treasure. We have cleaners come in, so my house smells like furniture polish and stale nothing. Good for Inga. Let her have all the fun getting her mail. I'm just getting out.

Next to my front door is a grandfather clock standing guard over a lacquered box where I put the mail so my parents can go through it in the fifteen minutes they're home. My own dining room is polished to a gleam, but never used. Our great room furniture languishes brand new and empty.

I throw my cell phone into the couch, hard. It's useless. No one would be calling to stop me.

No one had called me for three days. No text messages either. I figured that my absence from the bridge would cause questions, concerns, anything. And after what happened Sunday night, the thing that started my abstinence, I thought for sure Todd would call me. My best friend for more than a decade. But no, nothing. Inga now seems more like a friend to me.

My parents have big-time travel jobs. They make gobs of money, are very important, and are never home. It works out well for me. They're gone, so I don't have to deal with them much. My grades are good, so they don't have to deal with me.

Up the stairs, pictures of our smiling family on the wall leer at me. From the hallway, I hurl my backpack into my room, and then stand in the entryway of my parents' bedroom, wondering how I'm going to off myself.

A gun is your best bet, but my parents are anti-gun.

I storm through their immaculate room, more of a memorial than a bedroom, and into their spacious, gleaming white bathroom. I rip open the medicine cabinet.

Pills.

For the most part, pills are the cry-for-help suicide attempt. You take a bunch of pills that may or may not kill you, and then you have time to think. Of course you are going to have second thoughts. Then you call for help, they pump your stomach, and you wind up seeing someone professionally.

So with pills, you have to know the right stuff to take. Overdose on Tylenol? Come on. Classic cry-for-help. I can just see it. "Hello, 911? I ate a bottle of Flintstone's Chewables. I need help. I don't want to die." No, not for me.

I didn't want some pitiful failed suicide attempt that would trigger everyone's alarms. How miserable is the botched suicide attempt? Dang, you wake up, your body is all jacked up but you are still alive, hombre, with tears running down your pale cheeks. "I can't even kill myself right."

Please. God. No.

My parents don't even have leftover antibiotics. I do find one bottle of some prescription something, but again, I'm not going to try and kill myself with female hormone supplements.

They have safety razors, but I'm iffy on that whole slashing your wrist thing. Sounds dramatic, but I'm not a cutter. I have friends who are, but it's not my cup of blood.

I shudder down the steps and into the utility room. Kill yourself with simple household products. If people can make bombs out of lye soap, I should be able to find something to kill myself with.

In a cupboard, I'm digging through chemicals, reading labels. Get this, I have Drayno, and you'd think Drayno would do it, right? I mean, it eats through the organic material you have in your pipes. If I drank it, you'd think it would eat right through the organic material that is me. Well, no. Read the label. It tells you to drink milk, or whatever, not to immediately call the hospital.

It seems bleach is worse for you, but again, I drink a bunch of bleach, freak out, and wind up getting my stomach pumped and seeing someone professionally. No, I was going to go with a violent, completely sure way.

Hanging. If you can snap your neck with the initial fall, hanging's not so bad. If not, though, you strangle to death, and that just doesn't sound appealing. I would just have to chance it.

Out into the empty garage, I look for rope. Both my parents park their cars at the airport, so there's plenty of room to maneuver. I find some yellow nylon cord looped up under some jumper cables.

The problem with hanging yourself is where do you put the rope? I tear around through the inside of the house, but I can't find a good, stable anchor. Back in the garage, I figure I can get a rope

17

around a beam in the finished ceiling. I would have to saw through the drywall first, but that's not a big deal.

I'm in the attic, working, and I get that feeling again. I'm sawing through the drywall, watching my sweat lubricate the saw blade, but it seems like someone else is working. I'm just along for the ride, watching myself. Like I'm reading some whacked-out children's book.

See Jim saw.
See Jim hang.
Hang, Jim, hang.

I tie a knot that would make a Boy Scout grimace, and then thread the rope through the hole. I climb down the fold-up ladder, slowly. Like it's 1789 and I'm approaching the guillotine. "It is a far, far better thing…" Whatever.

I tug on the rope, even swing on it, and it holds. Back in the house, I get a chair from the kitchen table and slowly walk back into the garage. This is it. This is where my life ends.

What would I miss?

Not my parents' Cold War. They don't yell. They just stop talking, to each other, to me, to everyone. Except if they get a call from work.

Not getting up in the morning. There's this really cool song by the band Tool that talks about sleeping forever. About not wanting to stay sober. Every morning, I want to sleep forever. Like getting high. Every time I come down, I want to go up again.

I won't miss math and science homework.

I won't miss throwing up.

I won't miss always having to eat. Eating is a pain in the ass. But if you don't eat, when you do throw up from too much Jack Daniels, you throw up blood. *Nicht so gut.*

I won't miss boring Sunday afternoons.

I certainly won't miss my ex, Sylvia, who thrills herself by ignoring me. Nor my supposed best friend Todd being an asswipe. Three syllables. Ass-why-pay.

Above all, I won't miss Sunday night.

Death is better than Sunday night. Definitely.

Death is better than all of that.

Death is turning off the TV and sleeping forever.

I don't know how to make a noose, so I make a slipknot. Like the band. And I make sure there is no slack.

I climb up on the chair, and I look at the garage door, and I remember two things.

One, I don't have a suicide note.

Two, my dad. How will he feel, finding me swinging around in the garage when he drives in Friday night? My mom will be back on Saturday, so it'll be my dad. I don't want to do that to him.

My parents won't take my death well. I know. It'll push their teetering marriage over the edge. They'll blame themselves.

That's not what I want. It's not their fault that life sucks, that existence is a massive joke on our conscious minds. It isn't their fault I'm just done. So, the least I can do is not have them find me. I know I'll have to come up with a way for some cop to trip over my body, and then they can call my parents.

And I need a suicide note. A good suicide note that puts the blame for my suicide on either my own faulty design, or on God, who set things up like a moron with too many Legos.

Suddenly, killing myself seems like way too much work. That's the thing about suicidal depression. No motivation to do anything. I put all my suicide stuff away, go up to my room where I listen to Tool, the song "Sober," over and over, until I fall asleep. Probably around 8:30.

Why can't we sleep forever?

I wake up early, too early, and I realize that I have other things to do. Being suicidal means following a definite to-do list, and the first thing on my list is to get rid of all my stuff.

All of it. Where I'm going, I won't need it.

CHAPTER FIVE

IS THRIFT STORE FUN

My parents collect luggage like other people collect decorative plates. In the basement, they have all their cast-off bags and so packing up my clothes is easy. Good thing about packing for the end of things, wrinkles are not an issue. I just stuff it all in. I work fast, avoiding the temptation to look at my old t-shirts and go deep-sea diving into my old memories. My books I box up in cardboard from the garage. Again, I don't linger over the epic fantasy and mythologies because I know those are hooks trying to keep me tied to life. Not what I want.

I only need my laptop, for that ever-important suicide note, and my phone because every minute without my phone is torture. My books and binders from school, I can't throw away and I can't donate them to the Goodwill. I stack them on my barren desk.

I tear all my posters of bands and girls from my walls, leaving strings of paper and push pins. I like how ruined it all looks after

20

I'm done. My bedroom is now more prison cell than teenager sanctuary. I laugh at that. I'm just revealing the truth. I always felt locked up there anyway.

I trash all the mementos from my life with Todd and the bridge crew. The physical ones at least. Being a 21st century schizoid boy, my pictures, my music, my videos are all in my laptop and phone. Hell, I have e-copies of my favorite books as well. I think about wiping the hard drives, but that feels sooooo dramatic. No. Getting rid of my stuff makes sense, so my parents won't have to deal with it, and other people can enjoy my very black fashion sense. Anything else is too Jay Asher *Thirteen Reasons Why*.

I have only one reason. Life is not worth the pain.

I glance at the time on my phone. I can drop my stuff off at the Goodwill and still make it to school on time.

What? School? Why?

Let us return to my suicidal to-do list. I have to say goodbye to Todd and my friends, though I know I won't. Still, I don't have a suicide note, and I don't have a plan. Might as well keep up appearances until I can work all that out.

So off to school I go, talking of Michelangelo. Along the way I drop off two suitcases behind the Goodwill. Couldn't manage the boxes of books, but I can do that after school. My backpack is on my back, where it should be. Such a thing of beauty is my big, black backpack. I've written on every inch of it, writing in gold and silver marker scrawled with my favorite bands: Tool, Scattershot, Despair Nation, Gorge. The greats. Also, stupidly funny things Todd and my friends have said, and every so often, a poignant quote from some piece of fine literature.

I want to be buried in my backpack.

Then an idea roasts my brain. I'd give it to Todd before I left. A last grand gesture. Sure, but the problem is, I can't face Todd. Not after our Sunday night madness and my demonic interlude.

CHAPTER SIX

ME BABY, THE CHAPTER OF THE BEAST

School ends up being a monumental waste of time because I spend the whole day avoiding Todd and the other denizens of the bridge even though they are a high priority item on my suicidal to-do list. Worse than that, I wind up talking to the school counselor. Mrs. Farmer.

She has this round face, bobbed haircut, and she's deep into her forties, spelunking down into middle age. In front of her is a cup of old coffee, stinking like some horrific potpourri gone bad. Help-me-Jesus and Life-Is-Puppies books line the shelves and suck in the old coffee smell.

I sit down, wondering who tipped her off, and right away, I know what Mrs. Farmer wants.

She wants the magic answer. The silver bullet. Like the *Ordinary People* reason for wanting to kill myself, because I let my brother drown, or I was being molested, or something similar. Sad to say, I don't have any of the normal, I-can't-go-on-living problems. Sure, a bad night with my friends where I almost completely sold my soul to the Devil. Sure, my parents have a rocky marriage. Sure, my grandfather just died and I was ringside for most of his slide into insanity and death. But I have no easily diagnosed mental wound that she can apply a Freudian band-aid to.

When she doesn't get the silver bullet answer, she starts in with the normal questions, do I have a plan (kind of), do I have a note (none), have I been giving my stuff away (only to charity). I don't speak my parentheticals aloud. Then she asks it, "Jim, are you suicidal?"

"No, Mrs. Farmer, I am not." That little lie is the castle wall upon which I would make my stand. With the crucial question answered, she is relieved but still goes into the whole, this is all temporary, if you kill yourself now you'd be killing a stranger, things will change, life will get better, don't give up hope, keep hope alive, you're young, and you'll understand when you get older. Boils down to, "I tried to help you, and if you off yourself it's not my fault. Let me fling popcorn bits of wisdom at you until you go away."

Inga nearly got to me with a little of that rhetoric, but the school counselor fails miserably.

But thinking of my adventurous elderly neighbor gives me a question to ask. "What keeps you going, Mrs. Farmer?"

"Well, I have a daughter," she says.

I go unplugged and start saying a bunch of stuff I shouldn't. I know I have to be careful. One wrong move and she'd call EPS as in Emergency Psychiatric Services and I'd wind up in the clink. She was fishing for a reason to put me away on a 72 hour hold for a 5150. So very Van Halen, but without the Jack Daniels and fun. Yes, I'd answered the crucial question correctly, but still, I wasn't out of her clutches yet.

Words flow out of my mouth. "So you live for your kid. Okay, that's honorable, but I don't have kids, and if kids are going to chain me to this life, maybe I don't want any. It's stupid. People live for sex, and then they have kids, and then they live for their kids. We're nothing but salmon. No, salmon have it easy. They spawn and die. We just go on and on. If I had been born a salmon, I'd probably love life right now. But no, I had to go the Homo sapiens route, big frontal lobe which gives me hope and consciousness, two things God cursed us with, according to Friedrich Wilhelm Nietzsche."

I say all this stuff, and she gives me the aren't-you-clever smile, and then loses the smile to tell me about anti-depressants. "Well, there are medications you can take."

I snort. I can't help myself. "I've been, uh, self-medicating."

Then she sips from her coffee, which makes me want to puke, and says she called my dad, and recommended I see someone professionally.

She gives me forms for me and my parents to sign, the paperwork of the grand bureaucracy trying to keep poor Jim Dillenger alive. Great.

I am dismissed and sent back to class. Lucky me. I get to enjoy the last 20 minutes of my vector-sub-a physics class, worrying that I'll run into Todd. His last class is just down the hall from mine. I have to get out of there fast. Once I figure out the last details of my suicide, I can give him my backpack as a present, say goodbye, and cross him off my list.

In class, I count down the seconds. 5, 4, 3, 2, 1…last bell.

But Mr. Martin is still talking.

I panic. He's not going to let us go. In seconds, I'll be face to face with Todd, and I'm not ready for that.

I see someone in black walk past the window. Todd wears black. Must be Todd.

Then Mr. Martin lets us go.

That short delay is all it takes to screw up everything. If Todd is looking for me, he knows where to find me. I have to get away.

I hustle to the door, peek out. Coast is clear. Out I go. I wind my way through a sea of people until I get a glimpse of Todd, going against the flow, looking around, but not seeing me. I pick the first classroom I come to. Doorknob turns, and I'm inside.

And come face to face with Marianne Hartley. My savior.

Some of her friends are talking to the teacher around his desk, but Marianne is by the door. Right next to the door. Right there.

Marianne is in the genius classes like me, only she's a year younger, so we don't have much contact. She's home-school cute, with plain brown hair, inquisitive green eyes, a nice smile, and sensible brown shoes. No perfume. She's like the anti-Annie. I feel like an ink stain next to her. I wear black, have dyed black hair, just black. Not so much as a fashion statement or a memorial to the long history of rebels in black, but just because it's easier. Black matches everything, don't you know.

Her first words to me, ever. "I'm sorry."

"For what?"

She glances nervously at her friends across the room, then leans in close, and I smell soap. Soap amidst the classroom smell which is precisely one part book, one part dust, two parts hormonal, adolescent funk.

"I talked to Mrs. Farmer about you," she says, and her face glows with a blush.

I get this image of us making out, and I bet she would have that same color. It takes away most of my indignation and all of my breath.

"It was bound to happen," I say. "I mean, we all know the rules. If anyone talks about suicide, you have to take them seriously."

She laughs a little. "Yeah, I know. I was thinking about that all last night. I was worried. I'm so glad to see you."

"I'm not serious," I tell her in my best I-want-to-live voice.

She looks at me for a long time, and I know that the judge, jury and executioner haven't been convinced. Then she says, "Okay, tell me one good thing about life."

Everything I think of first I can't say. My first thought, sex. I know, I know, just a horny young man. Next thought, beer. Cracking open the first can of the night, the smell of hops and barley wafting out, the first sip, which signifies, "Life is good, and it's only going to get better." Next up on the list, the sulfur smell of the match after you light your cigarette. The gurgle of the bong. Marijuana incense smoking into your nose and straight into the very center of your cerebral cortex. Being with your friends at 3 a.m. when you're just starting to climb up out of the catatonia.

I stand there, not able to say any of what I'm thinking. Not to chaste and pretty Marianne Hartley.

"Is it that hard?" she asks in a quiet voice.

The way she says it, I feel like I'm some cute but horrible thing, the nice monster in a horror movie, twisted and wrecked, and she is the compassionate girl who will help me for a while, but then go off with the hero at the end. I feel her pitying me. It pisses me off.

I should yell at her, tell her that if she wanted to save my life, she should have sex with me. I should leave. I should do something, but I don't do anything. I just stand there, feeling lame.

She waits. Christianly and patient.

I finally say something. "Where do you live?" The words surprise her, like they surprise me.

"Rudyard and Ammons," she says.

It's walkable. Definitely walkable. I want to ask if I could walk her home, or if I could get a ride, or something like that. But I can't get the words out.

Her friends turn away from the teacher's desk. They're done. Marianne and I are done.

"Donuts." I try a smile, but it never reaches my face. "Donuts are good."

I give her a little wave, and then walk right out the door.

No one's in the hall. I keep moving.

Four days being clean. I have to get home before I find myself at the bridge, self-medicating, or talking to my old friends, or gazing at Annie's cleavage.

The yappy little dog isn't in its yard. Good. I'm not in the mood. All the way home, I'm trying to think of a plan, a note, working hard on my to-do list, but I'm just not inspired. I keep thinking about Marianne and her green eyes.

Damn that Mrs. Farmer, her kid, love and the ties that bind. Maybe what I feel for Marianne isn't love, but sex definitely ties you down to other people. I still feel shackled to Sylvia, my long-lost love.

Past the security guard, up the hill, and around the corner, and I pause in front of Inga's house. I go to the mailbox, check it, and there's mail in there. Great, now I have a big moral dilemma. Do I deliver the mail to her front door and rob her of her daily quest? Or do I let her get it? I sift through the ads and letters, which is probably a felony, and pick out what looks important. I'm assuming Inga doesn't need pizza coupons and gym memberships.

I see where I kicked the flower the day before, and I get a little guilty. I'd been pretty messed up, but still, no need to be a Visigoth. What did that flower ever do to me?

Ring, ring the doorbell. I hear Schatzi scratching the door on the other side, but no barking. What a cool dog he is.

I wait, listening to Schatzi whine, and I get nervous. What if Inga fell and never got up? What if her days of postal hijinks are over?

I ring the doorbell again, get out my phone, and get ready to call in the medical community.

"Please," I say, and surprise myself by feeling tears tickle my eyelids. "Just give me this one thing. Take me, not her. Please." I'm not praying because I don't know how to pray. I'm begging a world that doesn't care. Never did. Never will. To the universe, Ingalora Blute and the flower I kicked and your random ant are all the same thing.

Relief floods me when I hear the shuffle and cane. The door opens, and Inga grins at me. "James. I am very surprised to see you. Such a handsome young man visiting an older woman on her own. People will talk." Her "w's" come out as soft "v's". Adorable.

I blush. I don't handle flirting well. Not even with octogenarians. I did really well on the SAT's because I like words like that. I hand her the mail. "I brought you what I thought was important, but you still have ads and stuff in the mailbox if you want to make the journey today."

"So you went through my mail? Creepy."

I have to laugh at that. She's talking like she's my age and saying no to being my prom date. "Yeah, well, there's a fine line between stalking and helping."

"Thank you, James. I won't keep you. I'll make the very difficult journey later tonight and I'll use my cane."

A mental image hits me of her on the ground again. People would drive on by, since no one walks in Littleton except for me. "Hey, let me give you my cell phone number in case you fall again. You really should get one of those life alert necklaces."

She touches my hand. "Oh, no, James, but *danke schön*. The best part of any adventure is the uncertainty. I have become very creative in how I travel through life, and I have people to call. I don't want to be a bother, and there is your *Weltschmertz* to consider."

"There is that."

She gives me a last smile and withdraws. Closes the door.

What am I thinking? Trying to give her my cell phone number? I feel like the crown prince of creepy. Besides, I have work to do. A note, a plan. Instead, I end up doing homework. I'm such a hot nerdy mess.

My parents call me. I spend a whole bunch of time explaining that Mrs. Farmer and the establishment overreacted and that I'm fine, so fine, optimistic even. They buy it. Of course. They want to believe they gave me a gift when they gave me life. That I'd turn out like Inga, embracing the world and all the things in it.

Thinking of Inga, I can't help but compare myself to her. And I lose in the equation. I lose big time.

I force myself to stop pondering the old woman. Like I force myself to stop thinking about how hurt my parents will be from my suicide. I have to.

I need a cold heart. Instead, I get a donut on my desk.

CHAPTER SEVEN

HUNDRED MILLION CALORIES

Friday morning, I go to school in the same clothes I wore the day before. Maybe that's my plan, suicide by stink and social embarrassment.

I notice it right away. There's a donut on my desk in my English class. First class of the day.

"What's this?" I ask out loud.

"Looks like a donut," Cathy Hastings is kind enough to point out. She is a large girl who sits in front of me, and I spend a lot of time memorizing the back of her hair, and the mole she has on her neck. I call her ten sixty-six, like 1066 A.D., the Battle of Hastings. Never mind.

"Why, 1066, that is hilarious," I say and sit down.

It's a chocolate donut. A Winchell's donut, September of 2013, a very good year. I smell it. A fine bouquet. Grease and sugar. God so loved the world...

"Is it true, JD?" she asks me. One time she heard Todd call me JD, and so she thought it was the name I preferred. She's the only non-stoner-goth-freak to call me JD, but I figure it's only fair since I have a nickname for her. She's in every one of my classes. Always has been.

I take a bite. Heaven on earth. Could I live for donuts? Well, it works for Homer Simpson, so maybe I can give it a try.

"What's true, Ten?" I ask back.

She draws a finger across her throat.

"Do I look suicidal?"

She shrugs. "You do wear black."

"Good guys wear black," I say, knowing she's probably seen the bad action movie of the same bad name.

"You do your homework last night?" she asks.

"Yeah, but that doesn't mean anything. I just hate sitting in class all day long like an uninvited guest. I like it when they call on me and I know all the answers. Keeps those bastards on their toes." It's true. God help me, it's true. Here I am, suicidal and doing homework. Please. How can I bear the shame?

She turns in her seat and leans in close. She wears that cheap body spray, and I like it. It's so King Soopers. "I've thought about it," she whispers, and then gauges my reaction.

It doesn't surprise me. I mean, most people think about suicide, but few do it. It must be this inane survival instinct we all have. Fifty thousand years of trying to find something to eat doesn't just fade away once you can hit Taco Bell when you have the munchies. But for most of human history, at seventeen, you were halfway done with life. I could do another seventeen years. It's the last fifty after that which freaks me out.

"Don't do it, Ten," I say. "You'll meet your prince after high school and things will turn out all right."

High school, pre-class chatter fills up the room, and it drowns out our talk for a minute.

"I could say the same thing to you, JD," she says.

I shrug. No, no prince for me. Sex and love. Love and sex. It's a loser's game every time.

But I'm intrigued by 1066. "So you've thought about it, but what keeps you from dancing with the Devil in the pale moonlight?"

She gets this closed look. "I don't know. Maybe it's like you said. Life has to get better after high school, right?"

She wants to say something else, I can see that, but instead she's just giving me a line. What can 1066 be keeping from me? I mean, she's lived the social outcast life. Did she find the meaning in life by watching *Gossip Girl* or reading *Twilight?*

Weird, but I go along with her. Might as well give the fat girl some hope. "Right, Ten. After high school, it's all gonna be puppies, kitties, bunnies and sunshine. And rainbows." And Alzheimer's. And boredom. And disappointment. And disease. Somebody stop me.

The bell rings. Class begins, and I look at the mole on the back of 1066's neck. I bet she'll get it removed later in life. Good for her.

Then it hits me. If she knows about my own private suicide, who else does? And what big secret could she have? And why, when I'm looking for a reason to live, would she hand me such a lame line?

Life has to get better?

What a load of stupendous horsecrap. Life has a way of only getting worse in inexplicable ways.

CHAPTER EIGHT

GOES DOWN THE RABBIT HOLE

All day Friday the donuts don't stop.

Different donut for each class. Don't know how good girl Marianne knows where I sit, or how she figures out my schedule, but the weirdest thing is that I don't see her. I start to race through the halls, to get to my next class, to beat her, but I never can. How did she do it?

Maybe it's a little eerie-creepy. I eat them. I mean, a donut is a donut, but is she going to stalk me? Last thing a suicidal guy needs in the world is someone stalking them. I think about that during my lunch in the library, sneaking milk like I'm a hobo under a bridge guzzling Mad Dog 20/20 out of a paper bag. Had to keep the milk secret because you're not supposed to eat or drink in the library. Normally, I would have been with the stoner-goth-freaks, back around by the dumpsters, smoking cigarettes and talking trash...

talking trash by the dumpsters, never put the two together. Hmm. Garbage irony. Instead, I cool my brain in the library, baby.

Fifth period. A donut with sprinkles. I'm not much for sprinkles, but there's fried cake underneath them.

Sixth period, a note. In that girly handwriting. Biblical bad-ass Eve wrote in that same scrawling nice penmanship, I'll bet. Cleopatra, same thing. I bet Queen Elizabeth would write edicts with little smiley faces over the "i"'s. Here's the note. Short and sweet.

> Dear Jim,
> I have one more donut for you. Wait for me after class.
> MJH

Marianne J Hartley. Sure. MJH. I could call her MJ. My new Mary Jane.

But that pity stare, that charity gaze she gave me the day before—I don't like it. I don't want her to be my caseworker. The donuts all day long were cool. I did look forward to the next one, to see if I could catch her, but it still felt like stalking. Funny, her being nice to me made me want to kill myself all the more.

I would wait for her after school, and then I would unhinge and use my mouth to bring down her world, give her a huge dose of reality. Maybe I'd take a crowbar and pry the Jesus out of her heart.

I get meaner and blacker in my mind, waiting to destroy MJH.

The bell rings, and I see Todd outside the door closest to me, looking through the window. Todd has this pug face, like a beat-up dog, and his hair is naturally strawberry wispy, but he dyes it black, and it totally makes him look a thousand times more pale. And the freckles and the dye don't really match, but he's butt ugly anyway.

In the old days, Todd and I would've just loved to tear into MJH. Really explain the world to her. Make her suicidal.

But the old days are gone forever, and Todd is there to find out why.

He's the last person alive I want to talk to. Again, once the bell rings, I have this overwhelming desire to get home. I'm feeling motivated on the whole suicide note thing. I'd get to it, once I checked on Inga.

I join the throng of students leaving though the other door. I feel bad about not getting my last donut, my complete half dozen, but oh well. At least MJH won't feel my wrath for her being all Christian and nice to me.

And yet, there she is.

A chocolate éclair, on a flowery napkin, and she is smiling. She saved the best for last.

Todd will be through the room in a minute.

I march up and grab her arm, and get a little Jason Bourne for a minute. "Walk with me," I mumble under my breath, and she does, the éclair jiggling on the napkin. I grab it before it falls. We're around the corner, but not out of the woods.

Library is the safest bet. The bridge crew doesn't spend much time around books.

"Are you avoiding Brad?" she asks.

"No, I'm not avoiding anyone," I reply lamely. I'm not a good liar. For being a streetwise druggy, I'm sure not very cool. I feel compelled to do my homework, and I can't lie well. They keep revoking my juvenile delinquent ID card, and I have to fill out all this paperwork to get it back.

"Come on. I know a secret place," she says, and now I'm intrigued.

Here I was, going to tell her off, and I wind up following her through the gym, eating the last donut along the way. A good chocolate éclair truly is one of life's greatest gifts. Until the cardiac arrest rips apart your heart, and you wind up on a Rascal cart wheezing, with oxygen tubes stuffed in your nostrils.

No. Like everything else in life, even chocolate éclairs are an empty promise.

Marianne and I race around through the bleachers, and down a back staircase, and then to a door, which should be locked, but isn't. The door opens to another staircase leading straight down.

We could have just stopped in the gym. Not many of my old crew are very interested in push-ups and rope-climbs. Where are we going and why is she taking me there?

Alice down the rabbit hole. Curiouser and curiouser.

MJH doesn't pause, but goes straight down into the bowels of the school. I follow. Could it be I'm about to get lucky?

Around a sharp corner is a gymnasium storeroom. Mats, lacrosse sticks, football pads, ropes, pulleys, bows and arrows, a long aluminum slat off a bleacher. I feel like John Madden is going to pop out of a pile of football gear and say, "She's all yours, JD!" He'd have Todd's voice, of course.

I can't help but smile. MJH sees me grin.

She smiles back. Now we're getting somewhere.

"You said you wanted to hide, and no one comes here except me, I think. I come here when I feel like I'm drowning." She leans against some sort of cage, arms crossed.

One thing I got from Sylvia was how to read a girl's body language. It's a sad truth about this world, but I think most guys need a female to train them on all things female. And it can't be your mom. It has to be some hottie who eventually breaks your heart. At least that's how it worked for me.

So crossed arms is a bad sign, but what about the smile?

I stand there in silence, trying to use my female Rosetta Stone to unlock the secret of Marianne's cross-armed smile. I casually pick up a broken lacrosse stick. Two things she said have me thinking. She thinks I'm ducking Sutter. Okay, makes sense, after our little battle royale the other day. But what about her drowning comment? Dark. Too dark for Marianne Hartley, the good girl, the smart girl, the Christian girl. She can't have a dark side. Not with Jesus shining down on her.

"Are you feeling better?" she asks in a very counselor tone of voice.

I drop the lacrosse stick. "Listen, Marianne, thanks for the donuts and everything. And thanks for, uh, stopping the fight with Sutter, I guess, but I'm not what you think I am. I don't want…"

Your pity. Say your pity, Jimbo. I don't want your pity.

I don't say anything.

She has her nice, brown, sensible leather jacket on. It goes with her shoes. Nice and brown. "You don't want what?" Green eyes, alive and uncertain and excited. And that smile.

She waits for me to talk, and I know she is going to listen carefully to the next words I say.

"What do you want me to say?" That's what I ask her. *Smooth. Very smooth. Go get 'em, killer.*

"I don't know. Did you eat all the donuts?" she asks.

I walk across the room and lean up against a rough-edged cement wall. Getting closer to her. I'm going to call her bluff. Why else would the good girl invite me down into the basement of the school if she didn't want to dally on the dark side?

"Yes, I ate all the donuts," I say, "and you see, I'm diabetic, and I kept going into insulin shock, and it was only the sugar that kept me alive. You saved my life." It comes out bordering on poignant.

"So, no more suicide?"

She's leaning against the batting cage just a few feet from me.

"I was never serious," I say, and she just looks at me with those curious cat-green eyes. "Not that serious."

"Did you have a plan?" she asks.

I take a step toward her. Her arms cross a little tighter. Body language switches from ancient Babylonian to modern-day American, as in, "Uh, what are you doing?" The smile is gone. So gone.

There goes that. Might as well bail. I turn around and walk toward the stairs leading out to the world.

Might as well say anything because it all doesn't matter. "I'm thinking about hanging myself, but I don't have all the logistics down." I need a suicide note and for someone other than my parents to find me. Why did killing yourself have to be so complicated?

"Do you have a note?" she asks in that perfect therapist's voice. I bet she took some peer counseling course and I'm her first counselee. It sparks my rage.

"Hey, Marianne, thanks for everything, but I'm fine. Really. I don't need your donuts or your counseling, thank you very much."

She's unfazed. "Sure, Jim, do you think you're safe now?"

"Safe from everything except my own hand," I say with a little laugh. "I was just being paranoid. I was ducking Todd." Don't need to add Todd's last name. Everyone knows who Todd is.

"You and he were tight, I thought," she says. She still wants to talk.

I don't want to just walk out. I mean, it seems like we should walk out together. But she's not moving.

I'm not going to talk to her about Todd, or about my former life as a teen drug addict. Nothing like that. Not that I'm a drug addict. We've covered that.

"Marianne, I really have to get going."

That does it. We walk out in silence.

Out in the sunlight, we part.

I go to give her a wave, but she throws her arms around me and hugs me. My nose rests in her hair, and I smell her, and I melt. It's a long hug, and afterwards, I feel washed.

She gives me a shy, little smile. Flirty and hot. "Don't do anything I wouldn't do," she says.

That catches me, and I crack up a little. Blush. "Right. Thanks for the donuts." And we part.

Marianne and her mixed signals are too much to think about, and I try to turn it all off, but I still feel her body with every inch of my skin.

I walk through the empty school. Schools empty out fast, especially on a Friday afternoon. I should know that intuitively. It's school. No one wants to be there. But walking through the empty hallways, it's kind of melancholy. Schools are like parents, somehow, and when the kids leave, something is taken from them.

I take a deep breath. I'm a little shaky from the day full of donuts, but more than that, I'm shaky from Marianne's smell and touch. Well, who cares about all that? Friday night. I have the ultimate party to get ready for. My own death.

I do the normal walk home, but check Inga's mailbox. It's empty. She must have ransacked it while I was at school. I think about going to her and saying goodbye, but if I did that, she'd guess right away what I was up to. She's too smart for me to deal with, and so far, I don't have the authorities breathing down my neck. Just a form for my dad to sign, which would only be a piece of paper after I was gone.

In my prison cell of a room, I'm at my laptop, ready to type poetry and put my death squarely on God's own shoulders.

But then the phone calls start.

CHAPTER NINE

CIRCLES OF CELL PHONE HELL

It turns into the night of the cell phone. My mom, my dad and then Todd. Just three calls, but still, after nothing for a week, it feels like a lot. Nothing since Sunday night which I do not want to think about. Or talk about. Or deal with in any way other than avoid my old friends and stay clean. And kill myself over, maybe. Other than that, no big deal.

Mom first. I think about letting it go to voicemail, but I'm not writing anything anyway, so I might as well talk to Moms.

It's just chit-chat. She's in Cleveland, won't be home for a while, working on a big sale. She sells this hospital software. She's good at it, but she's gone a lot.

Mundane chatter, then she goes for it. "I know we talked about it on Thursday, but are you sure you're okay? This suicide thing has me concerned. Really, tell me, are you okay? Just be okay for one more week, and then you can fall apart."

Which do I respond to? Her first question, or the plea for me to not be a mess so she can close her big Cleveland deal? Please. Given the option, I would always go for what's behind door number two.

Funny, if she had just asked the first question, I might've answered her honestly.

I give her exactly what she wants. "Mom, I was just joking around, but someone told the counselor, and of course they have to cover their asses, or they could get sued. I'm fine."

"Are you sure?"

Of course she rewinds to what she had said, and now feels guilty, so she tries to offer me door number one. No way. She had her chance, and now I go castle wall on her.

"No, Mom, everything is fine. Again, they just blew it out of proportion."

She sighs. "I'm sorry, Jim. I'm sorry for everything."

Something is going on. My mom is one of those brutal, corporate gunslinger women who shoot first and ask questions later. She never apologizes. Or sighs. She's too busy ruling her end of the universe.

"Is everything all right with you?" I ask, uncertainly. Not used to asking my mom that particular question.

"Fine, Jim. Just fine. We'll talk. I gotta go." She pauses. She's probably answering her email. She then returns to me, her potentially suicidal son. Yeah, the email is probably more important.

"Okay, no problem," I say, and then it's the rote exchange of mother-son "I love you's" and we're done.

A second later my dad calls. He's an engineer for a software company, but he also works on the sales side. Also gone a lot. Sure, five o'clock on a Friday, both parents return to parenting for ten minutes before going back to their lives. Why do people have kids in the first place? It's such a pain in the ass. At least my parents were smart. They only had one.

"Jim, your mother and I talked earlier today, and we're both still worried. The counselor said we can't just ignore the situation, but we trust you. If you tell us you're okay, we'll believe you." Before I can respond, he goes on. My parents, two peas in a pod. "There were problems onsite, and it looks like I won't be home tonight. If it were any other client, I'd fly home, but I'll be home Sunday. Are you going to be all right until then?"

"I'm all right now," I say.

"But we're going to talk more on Sunday. Suicide is serious business." He pauses. "Things are going to change a little bit, but we'll get through it. Okay?"

"What's going on?" I ask. "Both you and Mom are going all CIA on me. Like all information is on a need-to-know basis. Well, I need to know."

"It's okay. We're all fine. No problems. Sunday, we'll talk a little more. No big whoop."

He's not going to come clean, so I don't even try. I get off the phone. Sunday they'll tell me what's going on. Sundays are becoming my least favorite day of the week.

I figure it's either about how they both are going to be working more, or they are going to be working less, so they can watch over me. Again, suicidal people do not do well under scrutiny. Leave us alone and let us die in peace.

The phone calls leave me shaken, unmotivated, disturbed at the impending disaster my parents are going to visit on me with their apologies and prophecies of change.

And then Todd calls, troubling my already oh-so-troubled mind.

CHAPTER TEN

DON'T CALL ME I'LL CALL YOU

"Yeah."

"Hey."

"What?"

"Dude."

It's almost like haiku.

> *Yeah hey what dude.*
> *Leaves lie thick on the stream.*
> *Friendship ends.*

Something like that, give or take a syllable.

I don't answer his dude. I just wait on the phone. Not sure why I picked up in the first place. I had this crazy idea that Marianne was going to call me, but I had checked the caller ID, so I knew who it was.

Todd talks and talks and fills the silence of his unanswered dude. "Uh, JD, I know things got weird on Sunday, and I figured I'd let you do your school thing during the week, but it's Friday night, and I'm sick of taking your name in vain. We were just on our way to Junky Pete's to score some KGB."

KGB. Killer green bud.

Oh God. Temptation nation.

"Annie's here." Todd throws that in. He adds a little laugh to it.

If I didn't say no, right then, I knew I never would. "Yeah. Go on without me."

Todd launches into it. "I didn't hear you right, JD, did I? You can't say no. No one says no to drugs. You say yes. When someone asks you, 'Mind splitting this bag of dope with me?' Then you say no, I don't mind at all. Else, you say yes. So, let me hear you say it."

"Todd, look, no, I can't."

"You going to stay home and commit suicide?"

How did the news get back to him? Todd isn't exactly at the epicenter of the Coyote Ridge High School community.

Like my parents, Todd doesn't let me answer. He just keeps talking. "And don't be freaking out about Sunday night. We were all teenage wastelanded, so we can't be held responsible for what happened. Besides, I saved the day because that's what I do. Super Todd. Faster than a bottle of Jack, more powerful than a locomotive full of meth, able to roll a joint in a single bound. I'll always be there to save your soul, man. So, are we good?"

Todd doesn't get it. Sunday night, yes, we had been drunk, stoned, fried, died, and laid to the side. Still, I about let something happen, something evil, something unforgiveable, when I could've stopped it. Todd stopped it, but I should have first.

He isn't the problem. I am. Down to the bloody foundations of my non-existent soul.

I throw him a bone. "Yeah, man, we're good."

"So…"

I'm in my room, laptop closed up. Every attempt at a suicide note was either too Sylvia Plath-y, or not enough. Before he called, I had Pink Floyd's *The Wall* all cued up on my phone. Music to slit your wrists by.

In the pause, Todd paints a picture. "We come over, pick your sorry ass up, hit Junky Pete's, come back here to Stoner Central and get lit up like Christmas trees on fire. What do you say?"

Some offer.

No way I'm going to go.

Todd's gospel goes on. "Listen, man, we've been friends for ten years. That's a full decade. If you're having a mind-bending bad time, let me snap you out of it. Let Super Todd save your ass. Okay?"

This isn't Todd. Todd isn't like this. But I have stopped being me. I guess that gives Todd permission to completely change his personality.

"So…" Todd says. He isn't getting off the phone.

And my resolve is weakening.

Go for Annie, I think to myself. At least with Annie, she isn't going to be looking at her therapist's watch, waiting for our hour to be over. She can give me more than just talk and donuts.

Or I can go to mark off the big goodbye-forever-here's-my-backpack item on my suicidal to-do list. Not there yet. I still love my backpack.

I don't go for Annie. I don't go to give Todd the great goodbye. No, I go because I want something from Todd and the bridge crew. Something that can save my life, if they can rise out of the mud of their drug addictions and teenage wastelandism.

"Okay," I say.

Todd laughs. It's not a happy sound.

CHAPTER ELEVEN

AGAIN WITH TODD
AND THE BRIDGE CREW JAMBOREE

Todd has a black Chevy Cavalier, only it's not really black, not anymore. It's kind of gray with dust and dings and white paint he dabbed on it from his summer job painting with his uncle. The car has only one real purpose. To drive us back and forth to Junky Pete's.

If we were older, we could've gone to a marijuana dispensary, complaining of glaucoma, but we weren't, and so we were stuck with old-school dope dealers.

Like always, it's full of people. Sylvia gives me a cold glance which is supposed to say we're friends, but doesn't. Ed, Fred, and Chad all hail my victorious return to the crew.

Todd, driving, gives me a big smile. He has something going on in there. Or maybe he's just glad he can still sway me so easily.

Was I going to smoke out, fall off the wagon, lose my six days of clean time? I'm not planning on it, but that's the thing, you don't usually plan on a relapse. They just kind of happen. Like most of the sex I've had in my life. Didn't plan on it, just kind of turned out that way. Lucky me. Literally.

I pile into the back, wondering where Annie is, but not asking.

Then we take off. Scattershot's speed metal thrashing guitars drown out all conversation so we yell.

"Where the hell you been all week, homie?" Todd screams from the front.

"Why didn't you call or text me to find out?" I'm on top of Ed, Fred, and Chad in the back, and we're a tangle of black clothes and limbs. All drenched in cheap cologne. It doesn't smell, really, just claws its way into the back of my throat. I'm glad for the cologne monster though, because of my clothing situation.

Todd grabs a beer can from his cup holder and drains it. "Am I my brother's keeper?"

Todd could easily do school. He could easily outclass me in all my snooty AP classes. He just lacked one thing. A sober brain cell. Just one is all that guy would need.

"Didn't your mother ever tell you not to drink and drive?" I yell.

"Who do you think taught me how to drink and drive?" he yells back.

"What about Mothers Against Drunk Drivers?"

"What about Drunks Against Mad Mothers?"

Everyone laughs. Even me. It's an old gag Todd and I have. But there's tension. We're sparring, I know it, even if Ed, Fred, Chad and Sylvia don't. And really, drinking and driving is all fun and games until someone loses an eye. Or you kill someone. I don't recommend it.

We roll up on Junky Pete's house and play Twister to get out of the car. Junky Pete resides in a duplex in search of a paint job, just across Rancho Carlito, the Denverish side of Littleton.

The chain link fence in front is so ancient and gray it looks as if a single touch would turn the links to ash. Through the fence, Junky Pete's grotesquely fat poodle looks at us lazily. Pete named the dog Jimi, like in Jimi Hendrix, then realized it was a girl at some point.

I should be walking side by side with Todd, but I wind up taking the rear. I stop and pet Pete's poodle. "Am I going to get through this, Jimi?" I ask the dog.

She looks up at me with mild eyes. It's the first time I ever pet her and didn't just laugh at her. She puts her chin on my hand, and I spend a long time just being with her, which makes us both feel a little better I think. If only the yappy dog had been like Jimi, or Schatzi, maybe I'd be less suicidal.

I give her a final scratch, and then walk right through the screen door. Fringe hangs like cobwebs on a bent frame.

Pete, as always, is on his couch. He takes up two cushions.

"Hey," he nods at me. Nodding. Junky Pete is good at that.

The coffee table in front of him is like a pharmaceutical company crossed with a Southern whiskey distiller's convention. Anyone could rob Junky Pete blind, if not for his girlfriend/wife, Melinda, supreme bitch queen of the multiverse.

She handles all the money.

She's always right there, standing in the ruined kitchen's doorway like an obese Colossus of Rhodes, her boobs fighting like angry twin boys under her violently pink sweatshirt.

Todd takes the chair next to Pete. The rest of us just sit around.

"I'm getting clean next week," Pete says. "Lose some weight. Get a real job."

Melinda barks. "No credit no more, you little bitches."

It's all drug-disjointed non-sequiturs. Pete always says the same thing. So does Melinda. We've always paid in cash, every time.

"We haven't seen JD all week long, Pete," Todd says, but this is more for me than for him.

Like a renaissance painter mixing colors, Pete starts dividing up the weed Todd's going to buy. "JD is right there," Pete says. "I heard things about him today."

"Really?" Todd asks. "What did you hear?" He gives me a look. Inexplicable.

Pete has these droopy dog eyes and a beard like thick dirt across his face. "Gobble came by." If Junky Pete is the god-king of our local addicts, Gobble is the crown prince. He's a low-life dealer who hangs around suburban supermarkets. A purveyor of illegal produce.

"Gobble said that he heard that JD was either going to get clean or commit suicide. He said he was worried he'd lose money if Jim quits. Or dies."

"I can't believe this," I mutter. "Does everyone know?"

Todd cackles. "I bet Morgue doesn't know, but once he takes a hit, he'll figure out his best customer up and died, and he'll be pissed. Live for him, JD. Morgue needs the money."

Morgue's a name you whisper, not say. He's a big-time dealer gangster lowlife who supplies the Denver Metro area with contraband. Rumor has it if Satan ever came down to earth, he'd ask Morgue advice on how to torture people.

Junky Pete tries to get fatherly. "JD, the best years of your existence lie ahead," he says and then adds, "I heard that in an AA meeting one time."

God, everyone knows about my suicidal malaise. Junky Pete, Gobble. Everyone. This is getting ridiculous.

All right, I ask my question. "So Pete, what keeps you going? You ever think about suicide?"

"This is so pathetic," Sylvia whispers, just loud enough for me to hear. She never did like me much. And I loved her so.

Pete looks at me through the veil of heroin. He even leans forward a little, as much as his stomach will let him. "Jim," he says, slurring even the bare syllable of my name. "I'm going to change. Life is good, Jim. Life is good." He leans back, as if he were Aristotle, finishing a thought.

We keep our eyes locked, and his eyes remind me of his dog out front. I then notice the white powder sprinkled on the belly of his *Master of Puppets* t-shirt. Not heroin or cocaine, but powdered sugar. From donuts. I see a yellow piece of processed dough to prove it.

He likes donuts. I like donuts.

Todd gives Melinda a roll of money, which she has to count, every time, twice. He then breaks into whatever connection Junky Pete and I had at that moment. "You really see Metallica in the clubs back in the 80s?"

Pete launches into his Metallica stories about how he saw them even before James Hetfield joined the group. Some other guy was the lead man for a while, but I'm not paying attention. I just stare at Junky Pete and the bookcase of philosophy books behind him. Was he one of my possible futures?

Like always, the same talk, the same interaction, weed and money are exchanged, and we take off, glad to leave. The car ride back to Todd's house is subdued as we all get ready to smoke dope, talk garbage irony, and get drunk.

Back at Todd's house, that's where the real fun begins.

CHAPTER TWELVE

ENDS

We cluster in the kitchen at Todd's house. It's like a ranch house, except the cows live in the house and the humans long for the barn. The carpet oozes in most places, sprinkled with bits and pieces of the world, in search of a good vacuum. Inexplicable holes dot the drywall. It's a place where dirty dishes and filthy laundry go to die.

In minutes the heavy smoke of mary-jew-awna fills the house. Good. Covers the stench of grossness from time immemorial. Liquor bottles strike the table with thuds and tinks, and the bong gurgles, and I feel like a coiled spring. They turn up heavy beat metal, Korn it sounds like. It drowns out everything, including coherent thought.

My feet keep wanting to leave, my head keeps wanting the smoke, and my heart feels like a pigeon in a cage.

Annie comes through the front door, a blonde, leathered goddess. She can give my life meaning. Instead, she gives me an icy look straight from the freezer and walks right by me.

"Annie, so glad you can make it!" Todd says in his loudest, stoniest voice. Eyelids at half- mast.

Annie's look is still clawing its way through my emotions. What happened? Wednesday she's all lovey, and Friday she looks at me like I'm raw meat. *Como?*

Sylvia breathes out a long string of smoke and hands me the bong. I take it and hold it like I had held my grandfather's hand, when he would reach out for help. Which was all the time.

I whisper a prayer to Inga. I don't believe in God. Might as well pray to a goddess.

The prayers to Inga help, and I pass the bong on down the line.

"Wait. Hold it. JD, you didn't take your turn. We bought enough for everyone."

Was this peer pressure? Yeah, it was. The dreaded peer pressure, famed peer pressure, the undisputed anti-hero of all anti-drug films.

Sylvia gives me the bong and it's Ed who gives me the lighter. I'm all set. Only a little hand motion and breathing keep me from dancing one more time with Mary Jane.

"Not tonight dear, I have a headache." I try to say it like a joke, only it comes out as a choke. I pass everything over to Ed.

Todd stumbles around the kitchen and winds up next to Annie. Who looks like she is made of marble. Angry marble. With his arm around her, he tries to gather enough sober thought to punish me with his dopey eyes. He finally talks. "Is it true what they say, JD? Are you a suicidal failure? Are you looking for the end? Are you a suicidal failure and is death your only friend?"

Suicidal Tendencies is the band. Todd is quoting their lyrics, kind of. He likes doing that. Most people find it annoying, but I always liked it. Not this time. Not right now.

I think everyone feels it. The tension that's been there all night is building to a crescendo. Ed holds the bong limply. He's let the cherry go out, which is a certified case of drug abuse

They're all looking at me, waiting for an answer.

I can lie. I can grab the bong from Ed and go back to them. I can just leave. I don't do any of those things. Instead, I tell the truth. I want to know if my closest friends can help me. My words feel like stone as I say them. "Yeah, I guess so. Can any of you give me a reason to live?"

It's like an awkward bomb goes off.

Annie is the only one who does anything. Her eyes fill with tears, she wrestles away from Todd, and storms out of the kitchen, down into the basement. Todd's room is in the basement. She probably winds up there on the mattress. Like Sylvia on Sunday night.

Speaking of which, my ex-girlfriend shakes her head. "You're such an asshole, JD. Annie's brother killed himself. You're such a selfish dick." She then follows Annie into the basement.

I'm left with my old buds. Todd, Ed, Fred, and Chad. Assonance at work.

"So that's what was with the laugh," I say to Todd. "I'd ask about Annie, and you'd laugh."

"Didn't have the heart to tell you in your condition," he says with a stony smile. "I'll comfort her for you."

That's why Todd invited me along. He and I had this girl competition thing, and I beat him every time. Like we both went for Sylvia and I got her. Ed, Fred, and Chad almost got her in the end as well, but not in any way Sylvia would have wanted.

Annie was all mine, until the suicide thing. Which Todd used perfectly in an attempt to win her over. Suddenly, I see Todd for what he is—poor, stoned, white trash, heading for a long life of worthless jobs and bar tabs.

Say what you will, but I can keep my focus. At that moment, I have nothing else going for me. "So why shouldn't I kill myself?"

Todd weaves through the kitchen, preaching his gospel. "JD, you said no to the bong. That's all there is, my friend. Sex, drugs, and

rock and roll. And I doubt you'll get any of those things from—"
pause to suck in a laugh "—Marianne Hartley."

He saw me earlier. He saw me with Marianne. I don't feel like I can
move. I stand frozen in his kitchen, all of them silently looking at me.

"So," I say. The music thuds into my guts, the snarling guitars
grind my intestines into chorizo. "So, to get through life, you run
away from life. I mean, it's all just for nothing. You always have to
sober up again. And you can't have sex forever."

Todd paces like something caged. He shouts over the music.
"Wrong! You're wrong! Every day! Every day! Every day!"

"Every day what?" I ask.

It's like we're on Main Street at noon, holstered pistols, cowboy
hats, and twitching fingers. Another fight. Another duel. The other
three guys look on, because the two best friends are about to gun
each other down.

Todd stops, obviously having forgotten what his "Every day!"
meant. He then narrows his eyes at me. "Homework, JD. It boils
down to homework."

"How's that?"

"You do homework, JD. We don't. You're in the AP classes, and
you'll go to college, and you'll become just like your parents. That's
why you're miserable. That's why you want to kill yourself. You see
what you'll become and you hate it."

I look at Todd. He reads every word out of my eyes, without me
saying a thing. His dad is just out of county jail, at a halfway house,
trying to get sober in AA. His mom works as a scheduling clerk in
a hospital, and she isn't home because she's looking for a bar guy
to bring home at 2:15 a.m. where they'll party with her son and
his friends. We all hate our parents, but at that moment, I prefer
mine—however absentee they might be.

I don't say anything. I don't need to.

"How come you said no to the bong?" he asks.

"Because of what happened Sunday night," I say. Might as well
kill the friendship by talking about what probably killed it. And

Sylvia is downstairs consoling poor Annie, so we don't have to worry about them hearing us.

"We didn't do anything," Chad protests.

I'm not sure if it's a complaint or a justification.

"But you guys would have." I stare down Chad, Fred, and Ed. They look away because they know I'm right.

Sunday night. We were all drunk and stoned on something a little extra, a little opium in the weed. Syliva passed out on Todd's mattress in the basement. With sheets and old blankets nailed to the unfinished ceiling, it's like a blanket fort for the deranged. Truth be told, it's cleaner than the rest of the house.

I remember we found Sylvia down there, me and the boys, but not Todd. He'd been upstairs, on the phone, talking to someone. Annie as it turned out.

Sylvia lay on the bed, completely gonerz, with her legs spread and a couple buttons on her blouse undone.

Chad chortled and said, "Look. Sylvia wants it. You know she does."

I didn't say a word. Last thing Sylvia was dreaming about was a bunch of stoned rapists abusing her.

Ed and Fred joined in the chortling. They went with Chad to the bed. And started to undress my ex-girlfriend.

And I remember thinking, *Good, she broke my heart. Let them break her body.*

I was going to watch every horrible moment because right then, lost in the haze of chemicals, I didn't care. I was someone who didn't care what happened to some helpless girl in the basement of some nowhere house. I even thought about using my phone to make my own twisted bit of porn.

Until Todd came bursting through the sheets, telling us that we were sick bastards and that he wasn't going to allow rape in his house because we were men, not animals.

Thank God for Todd. Thank the Devil for turning me into an uncaring, voyeuristic monster.

In Todd's kitchen, we don't talk about what happened, or almost happened. Don't need to. We all remember enough to feel ashamed.

Todd does this crazy little dance, head tilting. "It wasn't nothing. Super Todd stopped the bad boys from being bad. It's okay. It's all okay now."

"Still," I say.

Todd laughs, only it's not a laugh. It's filler. He then looks at me. He's trying to summon up the little clarity left in his smoky mind. "You didn't do anything, JD. These apes were the problem, but I whipped 'em back. You're fine, good, you're my boy, JD. So come back to the bong and we can pretend it was all just a bad dream."

No one moves. No one says anything. They are waiting for me.

I don't know what I'm going to say when I start talking, but I know I have to say something. "I want more out of life than getting high in your kitchen or under the bridge. And I don't want to be who I was on Sunday night. Todd, I didn't care what they were going to do to Sylvia. Do you get that? I didn't care. It was like I was a psychopath or something. A guy like that? He needs to die. If I can't change, I need to die. And if I can't fix this abyss inside me, I'm going to cut it out with a kitchen knife. Swear to God." I have no idea where all that came from, but it's true.

Ed, Fred and Chad say a bunch of stuff, about how they weren't really going to do anything, just undress her, but it's all lies.

They don't matter to me. Only Todd and I matter.

Todd returns my gaze through squinted eyes. I can see him make up his mind. "Well, if you want more out of life than our party, you are wasting your time. There is nothing but the party. And don't come slumming around, killing our buzz." Todd says it all in a clear voice that rings like a bell above the shouting music. "You may go. I dismiss you."

"Todd, I need more than the party. I need answers."

He smiles. "I dismiss you, James. You may go."

And like that, it's over.

§§

In seconds, I'm walking home to my empty house with nothing inside of me.

Nothing but the devouring abyss that feels like only death can fill.

CHAPTER THIRTEEN

REASONS WHY

I sleep. I don't sleep. I watch inane shows on my laptop, listening, then sleeping again. Not sure if I'm having trouble falling asleep, or if I'm having trouble staying awake. It all kind of gets mixed together.

Around four o'clock in the afternoon, I think it's time to get serious about my suicide note. I need the perfect music to inspire me.

I turn to Pink Floyd. It was Todd who pointed out that classic rock was classic stoner music. He got caught up in *Dark Side of the Moon*, or *Wish You Were Here*. I fell in love with *The Wall*.

"Comfortably Numb" is the *La Boheme* of suicide music. Like an SAT question. "Comfortably Numb" is to suicide as *La Boheme* is to opera.

I turn on *The Wall*, and in the darkness of my room, I listen to the whole thing. When the wall comes tearing down, I just lay there, looking up at my ceiling, in the ruins of my room. It strikes me that a movie about suicide wouldn't work. Pretty much, you would have a guy laying around, looking off into space, a tear sliding down his cheek every once in awhile. Not a lot of drama.

I'm that guy, looking off into space, feeling holes in my guts like so much Swiss cheese. I feel so empty it feels like the wind will blow right through me. The hole in my soul.

I'm going to do it. This is what people who kill themselves feel like right before they pull the trigger. Or right before they go on a shooting spree at their local high school. I'm not stupid or psychopathic enough to inflict my pain on innocent people. No, the school shootings are evil news. Just more proof God is either a mouth-breathing idiot or one gone guy.

I barely escaped the bong at Todd's. I think about what I said, about killing the person who I was on Sunday night. Only a matter of time before I get high again. I need to end such a monstrous life in a more permanent way.

Hanging is too complicated. I need a gun.

Todd's dad left a lot of guns in his house. I can patch things up with Todd, smoke some weed to prove he won, then get one of his dad's guns and shoot myself, right in his house. If anyone can handle finding my dead body, Todd can.

Marianne asked if I had a plan, and now I have one.

I get off my bed and smell myself. Ripe. I need new clothes because you can't kill yourself in stinky clothes. I know, petty and vain, but still, this is my big exit. I can't do it in a three-day-old outfit.

I decide to go to the Goodwill, buy some fresh clothes, then head over to Todd's. I'll bring my backpack and give it to him before I do the deed.

I pause at the door to my room. I have a plan, but I still need the perfect suicide note. Back at my laptop, my mind is blank. I want so much for the words to come, but nothing does. Nothing.

I want my suicide note to be profound, to wind up being printed in the newspaper. Morgan Freeman will read it out loud on the *Today* show. It will start a whole new initiative to stop teen suicide. To change society. To change the very nature of human life on earth.

Then news would come of my resurrection. Jim Dillenger lives! But only a perfect suicide note can change the world.

I make a quick list. All the reasons why life is not worth living. We've covered a few. Always having to eat. Math homework. Throwing up. Boring Sunday afternoons.

Those things are too simple and not noteworthy.

I think about my grandfather. He was this great, brilliant guy, a rocket scientist for real. And guess what life takes from him? His mind.

My first love, Sylvia Dickenson, my first everything. First loves should only end when you both breathe your last breath, in a final embrace that nothing, not even death, can shatter.

Parents should love each other.

Friends should always understand you and be there for you.

Kids should be safe from everything.

People shouldn't hate each other for their differences. Especially Christians.

People shouldn't starve to death, or die of AIDS, or be forever poor.

If there is a God, He/She/It/They should do more on earth.

Change shouldn't be so hard. Like Junky Pete, no way is that guy ever going to change.

I want my suicide note to be just like this one Pink Floyd song, "The Gunner's Dream" off *The Final Cut*. But if I'm reduced to quoting song lyrics, no way will Morgan Freeman be reading my last words on the *Today* show. Nothing will change.

I need time to think. After nearly twenty-four hours cooped up in my room, I need out.

I grab my coat, jam down the steps, and escape from my house. Thankfully I didn't give away my coat during my Thursday morning purge. In the end, I don't need it.

Outside, a warm wind is blowing through the cold air of the night. We get these autumn winds sometimes that forget summer is over. Add another thing for my list. Seasons should make sense, warm in the summer, cold in the winter, fall leaning toward chilly and spring heating things up. But no, it's all a stupid mix of temperatures.

The sound of the leaf chatter skittering over the sidewalk brings back times with Sylvia when I would walk to her house. Can't go see her. And since I don't have a suicide note, I can't go to Todd's and carry out my master plan.

Marianne. I haven't asked Marianne what snaps her out of the times when she feels like drowning. I haven't asked her why she goes on living. Maybe the sheer stupidity of her answer will help me with my suicide note.

"Don't do it, Jim. It's pathetic." I have to say the words out loud because I know I will ignore them if I just think them. "She'll think you're all weak and depressed and try and help you again."

"No, I'm going over to laugh at her. It's a perfectly legitimate reason to go and talk to her. It's all about the note now. All about the note."

"You don't know where she lives."

I'm being so difficult with myself. So I stop talking out loud. I'll find her house. Somehow, I know I will.

I check Inga's mailbox. It's full, so I sort a little and walk the important stuff to her front door. I ring the doorbell. No one answers. No Schatzi either, so I figure she must be out.

Inga's a trip. If only I had an ounce of her positive energy. Even a gram. I wonder how she got that way, but not sure how I can ask.

I then have an idea. I sling off my backpack, kneel, and grab a spiral notebook and a pen. I write her a quick note:

Dear Inga,

The other day we talked and you said your heart keeps you going. But how did you get to be so happy? How did you get to be the kind of person who sees life as an adventure? Even the simple things. I'm just curious.

Thanks.

James.

My note's not perfect. She hadn't wanted my cell phone number, so I'm not sure how she'll answer me, but I feel better for asking. Who knows? Maybe she has the perfect answer for me.

Probably not. Stupid me.

But I'm good at being stupid.

CHAPTER FOURTEEN

DIFFERENT ILLEGAL PHARMACEUTICALS

I remember to take in my own mail, so I return to my house and throw it into the box by the grandfather clock.

My belly gurgles. Dumb belly, always wanting to eat. I check the fridge and it's Old Mother Hubbard bare. My parents leave a credit card for food, so I scoop that bad boy up and head out. I'd need it to buy clothes anyway at the Goodwill.

So armed I'm back outside, moving down the sidewalk. Walking. Another thing that sucks about life.

You see, cops don't like it when you drink and drive. When you're underage, drunk, and driving, they all really hate that. When you're underage, drunk, only on a learner's permit, driving in a car that's not yours, well, they take away your license until your next life. They did mine.

Marianne said she lives near Rudyard and Ammons. Okay. Perfect. Goodwill and King Soopers and Starbucks all cluster around there.

I can hit the Starbucks for a big ol' Frappuccino, then King Soopers to load up on junk food, since I won't be living long enough to suffer the severe consequences of a poor diet. Fueled on caffeine and carcinogens, I'll sprint around the neighborhoods until I find the most Christian house on the block.

Silly me, but I feel almost giddy, tripping down the sidewalk. Jim Dillenger is going to make a night of it!

Pathetic. If I had the balls, I'd be dead already.

I walk past the kiddie bicycles out front and into the Goodwill. The place is full of yardsale rejects and dead people's clothes. Speaking of which, on the rack of pants I see one of my favorite pair of jeans. I grab them.

Ironically, I also find my favorite long-sleeved black tee. I sniff it suspiciously. Still Downy fresh.

Great, I'm buying back my own clothes. Underwear remains a problem. Target's a little further away, but I'd have to make a trip there eventually. Or stop wearing underwear. Things to ponder while you're trying to come up with a good suicide note.

They swipe the credit card, I sign my Dad's name, and then head over to the Starbucks to change in the bathroom. I wrap up my old clothes tight in a ball and walk out. No big deal.

Pretty sure the manager at the Starbucks hires Barbizon models because every one of his employees is smoking hot. All the luscious baristas behind the counter watch me walk up. I get all self-conscious and forget about the Frappuccino. Instead, I get a venti white chocolate peppermint mocha. It's like French kissing one of Santa's elves.

I pay and they smile. I try and smile back, but I'm feeling embarrassed. Wearing my own clothes I had to buy from the Goodwill doesn't exactly fill me with confidence. Besides, those girls glow too brightly for me to think I had a shot at them.

Outside, I suck on the coffee. The sugar and fat calm me down. I toss my old clothes in the dumpster.

Got my coffee. Now I needed a bag of Nacho Doritos and some beef jerky and I'd be ready for the Olympics. Saturday night traffic is all happy and partying at the stoplight. Even the families with kids raiding the McDonald's Redbox seem to be celebrating.

Everybody is so frickin' happy. Good for them.

I cross the intersection and walk through the packed parking lot toward the grocery store.

In front of the King Soopers, Gobble is there selling drugs to housewives. He's trying to act casual, with his hands in the pockets of his ankle-length trench coat. Chains, random metal bits, and cryptic writing cover his clothes—jeans, shirt, and coat all equally bejeweled.

Gobble has a waddle of fat and skin hanging off his chin, which makes him look like a turkey. His hooked nose and bloodshot eyes don't help. His hair shines with grease. He's like the Greek god of ugly.

I go to walk by, not wanting his drama, but he stops me. "JD, man, is that you? Dude, are you really gonna off yourself?"

"Hey, Gobble," I say. "I got me a mocha. People who drink mochas don't commit suicide."

Such philosophy catches him off guard. "Really?" His eyes tell me he's not functioning within normal parameters.

I shake my head, try and leave, but not before Gobble gives me his best sales pitch. "JD, I have some Oxy. You want it? My customer stood me up. And my usuals aren't here, not on a Saturday night. Weekday mornings, after morning carpool, that's when business is good."

Depressing. Mothers taking drugs. I have to close my eyes. Why did the world have to be such a mess? And who in their right mind would buy dangerous chemicals from someone like Gobble? Desperate people. I'd come shopping at Gobble's trenchcoat storefront before.

"You okay?" Gobble asks. "You don't look so good."

"No Oxy for me, Gobble. I'm good."

He leans in closer. Great. Now I can smell his breath. Lucky, lucky me. "What about other stuff? I got OxyContin, Percocet, Percodan…"

"That's all Oxy, Gobble. Come on. I gotta go."

"Valium? Vicodin?"

"What's with all the pills?" I ask. Gobble is usually far less a pharmacy and more of a farmer's market.

He glances around, leans closer. Ew. "Had a customer who got clean in Narcotics Anonymous. I bought out her medicine cabinet. I got some Lipitor."

"That would lower my cholesterol," I say, "and I have big plans to send it skyrocketing. Good luck, Gobble, but I'd wait until Monday morning. And try to avoid the cops. A fine-lookin' man such as yourself wouldn't last a day in prison."

He blinks. Like a November turkey. I leave him blinking.

He's gone when I emerge with my industrial-sized bag of Doritos and my satchel of beef jerky.

Now, to find Marianne Hartley, make her explain herself to me, and then go back home, write my note, go to Todd's, and blow my brains out.

A busy, busy night lies ahead of me.

Past the King Soopers, walking down the sidewalk, I pick a side street, walk to a corner, walk to another, then another. In moments, I'm lost, surrounded by a million houses. Lights are on in the darkness, happy little families watching TV inside. The houses are all different, and the trees are big, full and majestic—cottonwoods leaking cotton fluffs and stately birches, so different from the weedy aspens in my neighborhood. Some of the lawns are a little rough around the edges with bikes and Big Wheels parked haphazardly about, but that's okay. It's a nice, established place. A good place to raise kids and watch them grow. A place for tree swings and Sunday brunch.

Makes me even more depressed. I finally sit down on the curb to eat jerky and tortilla chips. Chase it down with slurps from my sippy-cup Starbucks.

Feet in the gutter, I alternate from anger to despair. Miles of houses. So dumb of me to think I could ever find her. My little quest for Marianne ends in disappointment. Really? I'm so shocked.

I'll have to wait until Monday to talk to her, to ask her about her drowning times, but I know I can't wait that long.

Despite the warm wind, I shiver from the cold inside. I feel nauseated from the cheap meat and cheaper carbohydrates.

This is why I want to die.

In a perfect world, when you go looking for a girl in your corner of a labyrinthine suburban hell, you will find her, even if you only have the intersection. If God wanted to help me, he would've helped me find Marianne's house. I need a miracle, and of course heaven is silent.

I get up to go home. A car slides by me and turns into a driveway right where I was sitting. Then I hear it.

"Jim?"

Careful what you wish for.

It's Marianne and her cheerful, guitar-wielding, kumbaya-singing pack of wild-eyed Christian friends.

And me. Dressed in black. Hating their God.

CHAPTER FIFTEEN

WITH LIONS AND CHRISTIANS AND SWEET MARIANNE, OH MY

On the sidewalk, my feet first point in one direction and then another. I stuff the beef jerky packaging into the Doritos bag, then try and roll up the bag, but it doesn't get very small. Embarrassing.

Marianne runs from the car, all concerned. "Jim, what are you doing here? Are you okay?"

"Hey." I put up a hand. It's orangey with Doritos dye. I know, hot, right?

I take in Marianne's house, obviously hers because the place is so wholesome. A front porch complete with a porch swing, a big cottonwood out front with the perfect limb for a tree swing, and twin pine trees flanking the whole two-story, well-painted structure. Christmasville in Littleton.

While I'm thinking cozy thoughts about Marianne and her perfect life, the Christians walk up behind her. You know they are Christians by their love, by their love, yes, you know they are Christians by their love. We're standing under the streetlight, on the corner, in front of Marianne's house. There's five of them. Young to youngish.

She introduces me around. I nod and try to act like I don't want to dribble down into a puddle and trickle away into the gutters.

Instead of running away, I ask, "Hey, Marianne, can I talk to you alone for a minute?"

One guy with a little ghost of a goatee answers for all of them I guess. "Hey, sure, no problem. No sweat. Sure." Do I sense that he doth protest too much? Is he sweet on Marianne? Instantly, I hate the bastard.

Then he does it. "Hey Marianne, is this the guy you told us about?"

Marianne turns the color of snow on paper. She downright blanches. Maybe even bleaches.

"Uh, Doug," Marianne says.

Some names are just bad news. Like Lacey. I've never met a Lacey I've liked. And here's Doug. Dougs are all bad news. Like Rodney. Rodney is going to rip you off and steal your girlfriend. They can't help it. It's in the name.

Her "Uh, Doug" should have stopped him.

"I used to wear black and hate life," Doug is saying, completely killing Marianne. "But then things changed."

Anger breaks through the misery and despair of my Pink Floyd evening. "Let me guess, Doug, you accepted Jesus Christ as your personal savior. Is that about right?"

Doug takes defense, but there's a definite devilish edge to him. "Yeah, something like that, but the point is I don't want to kill myself anymore. Can you say the same thing?"

"Religion, the opiate of the masses," I say. "Let me break it down for you—"

He cuts me off. "I get it, religion is just another drug," he says, and I see him calm himself down. I'm squared off, one more time, another fight, only this one isn't going to end up with me getting my ass kicked. I don't think. But I don't know. You never can tell with those wacky Christians.

I size him up. He's older, graduated, probably going to MIT, Metro In Town, as in Denver Metropolitan College. Okay, let's get it on. "Okay, man, let's assume there is a God and that religion isn't totally worthless. Well, He gave me my life, right? I'm just giving it back to Him a little early."

"Life is a gift, man," Doug says. "Jesus died for your sins, and if you just kill yourself, it means you don't give a shit about what He did."

Ah, a Christian who curses. The very best kind. The only kind I like. Maybe Doug isn't so bad. But I'm going to school him anyway. "So God created the world, right?"

"Yeah." He says it like it's a big concession.

"God created me, right?"

"Yeah."

I can sense the weird energy. It feels like a fight. An honest-to-goodness fight. We even have a crowd.

So I go in for the ol' one two. "So if God created me, knowing that I was going to grow up and hate life and kill myself, then how can God blame me when it was His shoddy design? It's His screw-up, not mine. I'm just doing what I was created to do."

Stick that in your tailpipe, DDDDDUUUUGGGG.

"Free will. You were created perfect, and what you choose to do with your life has consequences." He then pauses. "What you think you practice, what you practice you become, and what you become has consequences."

I kinda dig that. I kinda dig what DUG had to say. I think about saying that, but we're into it, and he countered my right cross.

"I'll take a certain amount of responsibility, Doug, for my actions and my current state of despair. But I don't think God can just wash His hands of me. He has to take some responsibility too, and the way I see it, He hasn't."

"That's what Jesus is for," Doug answers. "Jesus was the sacrifice for—"

I smile broadly. "For God's imperfect creation. God screws the pooch creating our world, and then kills His own son to make up for it. And now, why do I want to be part of a religion like that?"

"No," Doug starts to say, but I'm not done.

"And speaking of suicide, Jesus killed himself. I mean, if He's the Son of God, and He has unlimited power at His fingertips, He could have fried those Roman soldiers like the last scene in *Raiders of the Lost Arc*. Only, He doesn't. He lets the Romans kill Him. That's suicide."

One of the girls breaks in. "Doug, I have a curfew. I have to get home."

Curfew? Wow, she must have parents in the same state. So this is how the other half lives.

Doug puts out a fist. I'm supposed to bump fists. I do. God help me, I do. He's not so bad.

Doug smiles. "We'll talk more, Jim. You have a good head on your shoulders. There's hope. Never give up hope."

They wave with pity in their eyes, and I'm not sure if they are waving at me or poor Marianne, who is stuck with me.

They pile back into the car and take off.

"Awkward," Marianne says. "Listen, it's not like I'm telling everyone. At youth group tonight, we talked about suicide, and I thought of you."

I should be pissed, but I'm not. I do want to cut to the chase, though. "Marianne, yesterday, you said sometimes you feel like you're drowning. How do you get out of that space when you're in it?"

Marianne looks up at her house, a kind of nervous glance. "We should probably walk or something. My parents might come out. If they heard the car…"

Her parents are in the same state as well. Maybe it's catching.

We walk.

No moon, it's dark, but then it's the suburbs so it's never really dark. Houselights and streetlights give everything an atomic orange color. Very nacho cheese. Like the bag of chips I'm carrying.

Marianne walks with her hands in her brown leather coat. "I don't know, Jim. I think about God." Her voice gets funny. She's embarrassed, and I don't want to embarrass her, and I don't want to spar with her.

Okay, gotta ease her down. "Hey, Marianne, Doug was trying to convert me, and I hate that. I just want to hear about you, not about what the world should be doing, or what I need to do. I'm not going to jump on you."

Unless you want me to, I add in my head. Marianne is cute. Maybe not that cigarette-slutty cute that Annie has, but more of a wholesome, apple-pie cute. And suddenly, I don't want to laugh at her answer. Suddenly, I'm curious.

She shakes her head. "I'm sorry he got all Jesus-y on you."

I shrug. "Keep going. What about this whole God thing helps you out?"

She lets out a long breath. "Well, I agree with Doug, I guess. Life is a gift, only it's like a gift that you have to give away to really enjoy. Did I say I sometimes feel like drowning?"

"Yeah."

She shakes her head. "I can't believe I would've said that. I never talk to people about that. But it's true. Sometimes it all feels like too much. It's like other people, like Doug I guess, seem to know exactly what is going on, and I feel lost, all the time. But then I think about what I can do for other people. I think that's what being Christian is about. Helping other people. That's what Jesus wanted us to do. Not be saved, or whatever."

"So you buy people donuts?" I ask, trying not to be mean, but I knew it. I'm her project.

She nods. "Yeah."

I can't help it. I got my answer, and now I want to argue with her. "But that means it's still selfish. It means you are doing it to make yourself feel better."

"I guess so," she says, and sure, it's a victory, sure, I beat her, but it doesn't help me. Talk about a Pyrrhic victory. I win, and I get to keep all of my misery. She loses, but at least she's content.

71

She turns on me. Her voice gets jagged and angry, and I like that. "But so what? I never said that I wanted to be a saint. Trust me, I'm not. I try to help people when I feel like nothing matters and life is a joke. And it helps me. And I think it helps other people. So who cares if it's selfish? Maybe it's a good selfish."

Point well taken.

We walk in silence. The whole day, the whole week, is weighing heavy, and at that point, I don't care if I live or die. My care button is broken. I'm just a crutch she uses to make herself feel better. Might as well say anything to her. Nothing matters anyway.

"Well, Marianne, if you're looking for a charitable cause, you could sleep with me, because hey, it's been awhile. And trust me, it would really, really help me out."

I expect vitriol. I expect a slap. I expect anything but her laughter.

"Sure, Jim. Right here. Right now. Better yet, I'll sneak you up to my room, and you can have your way with me."

I stop walking. My mouth drops open. "What?"

Then she really laughs. "Talk about calling your bluff! I gotta get home, Jim. Let's turn around."

We swivel and head back down her block. I'm silenced.

"Besides, Jim, I don't date guys with one foot in the grave. I don't look good in black." Good quip. Funny. I'm liking Marianne more than I should.

My mind keeps going back to what she said. What helps her go on. Food for thought. We talk. We chat. She gets the keys from her parents, and she drives me home in their SUV. Good. I was worried the Minotaur of her suburban labyrinth would jump out and eat me.

She pulls up in front of my house and it looks haunted. Sitting there, I realize how much I don't want to spend another night alone in my house. The trees are so thin. I want huge cottonwoods spreading above me, blocking out the sky.

She doesn't say anything, and I'm thinking I have a chance at a kiss.

I turn to her and wait for it. That's the secret to the kiss. You wait. You wait and gauge the situation and the girl. Every girl and every situation is different, but you can figure it all out if you just wait. If the girl puts out a hand, well, homie, you're done. A handshake. Dang. Or that yoga-like-over-the-emergency-brake hug. No good. But if you wait, and you lean in, and there's the pull, then you got it, ace.

In the wait, in the pause, she shoots me down.

"We'll talk on Monday, okay?"

Words mean no kiss. Words are just words.

"Sure," and I throw a little salute at her and get out.

I watch her drive off. I can still smell her in the night. It feels like the end of a date, and that by no means is a bad thing, kiss or no kiss.

Out of habit, I check the mailbox, though I know it's empty. It's not. In it is a piece of stationary with flowers on the border.

Inga left me an answer.

CHAPTER SIXTEEN

THE CONFERENCE CALL TO END ALL CONFERENCE CALLS WITH THE PARENTS

I grab the note and read it while sitting at the kitchen table. I know I'm not going to Todd's house, and I also know my suicide note isn't going to happen, not that night. Not while visions of Marianne dance like sugar-plums around in my head.

In her note, Inga throws in some bitter candy to consider.

Dear James,
I was so surprised to get your note. Very old-fashioned of you. I have friends who insist on using the email, but computers and I shall never be anything more than distant acquaintances.
As for my current state, do not let my optimism and cheerful demeanor fool you. I've wrestled with my own Weltschmertz all my life, and you've happened to catch me on a good year. For long periods of time, I have been caged in depression.

Not to bore you, but I grew up outside of Dachau. As you know, it was a death camp during World War II. When I was a girl, I would watch the trains come, filled with people, on their way to die. I could see the smoke from the fires. I could smell it, James.

There is a darkness in this world. I have seen it. I have smelled it. But we'd both be fools to think that means there is no light.

For me, I have to have a purpose. If I feel useless, I die. People don't rust like unused tools. Unused people crumble apart from the inside. If your Weltschmertz is keen, find a purpose.

Your note has made me ramble. Now I have bored you. I shall stop writing. I wish you purpose and peace.

Your friend,

Ingalora

I can't get up from the table for a long time. Leave it to Inga to pull out the big guns. The Holocaust. What is my life compared to that? The guilt makes me feel worse and suddenly I'm so tired. I need a break from my mind.

More sleep. Large amounts of sleep. Bliss. That Tool band, those guys are brilliant. Why can't we sleep forever?

I give it my best shot.

I wake up the next morning, well, morningish. Crack of noon. You get the picture. Lying in bed, I ponder the twin philosophies of Inga and Marianne. They are basically saying the same thing. I need to find a purpose. I need to try and help other people. But Marianne's argument goes deeper. Life is a gift, but it only feels like a gift if you give it away.

Makes sense. If you hate your life and are suicidal, you might as well go work with the poorest of the poor because nothing really matters, and you could do some good for others since your life sucks so much.

It's the backend of the crime-wave suicide argument. If you're suicidal anyway, you might as well steal a bunch of money and live large because you're going to die anyway.

Both arguments are flawed because of the simple fact of suicidal depression. I can't even find the motivation to take a shower. The last thing in the world I want is to fly to Calcutta and have people puke on me. And pulling a bank robbery takes way too much effort.

I turn over in my bed and close my eyes. I'm kidding myself. After fourteen hours, I'm done sleeping. But I have nothing better to do. My pool of friends has shrunk to a puddle. 1066 is just an acquaintance. Marianne is just using me to make herself feel better. I'm her giant, black pacifier.

Then my dad gets home and things get worse.

He comes in and sees my eyes. He can tell right away something is off.

"Are you okay?" he asks me and plunks down his suitcase in the living room.

"Yeah, why?"

"Did you get any sleep last night?" my dad asks.

"Yeah." Enter laconic teenager. I don't know how to tell him that Todd and I broke up. That's what it is. I'm not gay or anything, but that's what happened Friday night. Both my folks will be overjoyed. They don't care much for Todd. Wrong side of the suburb, I guess. East of Rancho Carlito, things get a little ghetto-y.

My dad looks at his watch, which for my parents, is akin to breathing. It's what they call in the science world, an autonomic response. No higher brain function needed.

"Your mom is going to join us on speaker phone."

I sigh. I can't help it. Only my parents would announce whatever terrible thing they have to say via conference call. Right in the middle of my suicidal malaise.

Dial tones and numbers, and there's my virtual mommy, talking out of my dad's smart phone. Man, the whole world takes place in kitchens. Houses should just be kitchens with bedrooms attached and a home theatre in the basement.

"Hi, Jim, how are you feeling? Better I hope." My mom doesn't ask me, but tells me.

"Yeah, better." I say.

My dad lets out a long breath and starts. "Jim, you know things haven't been going well with your mom and me. With her job being in Cleveland, we're going to separate for a while, to see if we can work things out."

At that moment, I don't know what I'm going to say. I feel like an upside-down Empire State Building is balancing its point right on the center of my skull.

"Jim, sweetie, don't blame yourself. There's nothing you could have done." This from Mom who probably studied up on how to talk to your teenager about divorce.

"This shouldn't come as a shock to you," my dad says, appraising me.

I shrug and crave a bong hit so hard I can almost taste the smoke in my mouth, and the joyful gurgle of the smoke on the water. Cue Deep Purple.

"I told you we should've done this over a video conference. I can't see his face," my mom says abruptly, probably to fill the silence.

"I could load the Skype app," my dad offers.

My mom's sigh comes out as static. "Too late for that now."

"Say something, Jim," my dad says, and I see the guilt.

I'm glad he didn't come home to see me swinging like a cattle rustler in our garage. It would've killed him too.

So I say something. "I knew it was coming. But I don't see how you're going to work it out if you're both in separate states. Why don't you just get a divorce and end it here? What's the point of dragging it out?"

"He's a bright kid, Chris," my mom says to my dad.

They both start to talk, and my mom wins. As usual.

"We are talking to our attorneys, Jim," she says. "We just wanted to ease you into the idea."

That pisses me off. Big surprise. "Yeah, I'm so bright. Sure, I saw this coming. I bet you both did too. It seems to me, you could have done more, but I don't know. Divorce each other, hate each other, whatever. Can I go now?" I'm surprised at the words, and oh

God, tears are in my eyes. Not what I wanted. Not how I wanted to react.

"We did try," they both say together.

"Jim, I'm sorry," my dad says. Tears are in his eyes as well, which for a Lockheed engineer probably means a dock in pay.

"Jim, it's not final. Nothing is final. Yes, we are thinking about getting a divorce, but…" Moms was throwing me a bone.

I don't want it.

"So what's the point?"

"Come again?" my dad asks, but I know he knows what I want.

I wipe a tear off my face. "I mean, what's the point of any of this? You're getting a divorce, and that's pretty much how marriage ends. So there's no forever love, or whatever you want to call it. I'll be going away to college next year, so I guess it's a good time. Have kids, get divorced, die." I don't add all Alzheimered out in a nursing home, but I bet they both can hear what I don't say.

Then my mom utters words that mean absolutely nothing. "You'll understand when you're older, sweetie. I'm sorry this is hard for you."

I shut up, shut down, hard. I cross my arms, sit at the table, and let them chatter, but I'm done.

My mom finally gets off the phone, and it's just my dad and I.

With her gone, I feel more free to talk. There's less of a chance my dad will tell me how to feel and what to think.

I aim my favorite question at my dad. "How come you go on living?"

He leans back in his chair, and runs a hand through his thinning hair. My dad is still a good-looking guy at fifty. I will probably age like him, though aging is not a priority for me.

He looks at me. "Is this about that phone call from school, Jim? Oh and I signed the forms. Can you bring them to her tomorrow?"

"Sure. But what about your answer? Since everyone thinks I'm suicidal, I've been trying to find out what keeps people going. Like a sociological experiment."

"Well," he says slowly, "you have to find your own answers. I guess that's what life is all about."

Not bad. He says I need to find my own answers, and Inga says I need to find a purpose. I want more, so I press him. "What are your answers, Dad?"

"I guess my problem is that I get caught up in the day-to-day stuff. I don't think about it. I like my work. I find it interesting. I try to be a good husband and father…" He can't go on after that bunch of irony about being a good husband. I know my dad. He blames himself. For just about everything.

I'm feeling mean again. My tears are all dried up. "Dad, you work at Lockheed, which makes missiles. So your life is about killing other people."

That makes him laugh. "I never thought about it that way. No, it's not just about work."

But it is, dad. You know it is.

"Quit," I say. "We'll go live in Cleveland. You and mom can give it a real shot. I pretty much don't have any friends here anymore."

"What happened with Todd?"

I wave my hand over the table, like I'm making the last decade of my life disappear. "Quitsville."

I see him relax with relief. Then he tenses up and gives me a line of total garbage. "It's not that easy, Jim. I mean, I could retire in eight years. And I'm not sure if staying together is what your mom really wants."

I stand up. "Eight years is a long time."

He looks up at me. "We'll get through this."

He might, but I'm not planning on it. Nope. Not this hombre.

"Sure." I give him the useless word, and then go up to my room and play out my life, one more time in my head.

A boring job I'm chained to, kids who are broken, a marriage just as broken, and a long decline into a troubled death. Inga is wrong. In the end, we have no purpose. Life doesn't mean anything.

Marianne's face comes back to me—pensive, in the shadows of the night, under a streetlamp, with a warm wind blowing from nowhere.

I ask her non-presence, "What do I have to give, Marianne? What can I do if life has no meaning?"

She isn't there to answer. Probably hanging out with DUG.

I go to bed at seven and sleep until the next miserable day starts.

New days always come. Always.

Unless they don't.

CHAPTER SEVENTEEN

WITH TWO GIRLS JUST OUT OF REACH

First period of the day, 1066 turns around. I give her a long withering look. I'm in Saturday's clothes and the same underwear since Thursday. I want to die.

Mrs. Farmer has her signed form saying she told my parents I'm suicidal, or at least I talked about it. Her life is now complete. Where's my signed form saying God made a huge mistake giving human beings consciousness and hope?

1066 appraises me. "It's true."

I'm too gone for words. I just squint at her. What is she talking about?

From her stuffed backpack, she pulls out a little paper bag. A donut. Winchell's.

I have to work my mouth a few minutes to get my face going until I'm ready for actual speech. "What's that?" I ask.

And then a thermos comes out of the backpack. She has a little paper cup, and she tries to balance it on my desk, but the desk is sloped, and it skitters toward the edge, which annoys the hell out of me. Desk. Sloped. Good for writing. Bad for pouring.

It's coffee.

I have to smile. I have to. 1066 drags it out of me.

"I figured today might be rough for you," she says. "And you look like you need a cup of coffee. A little pick-me-up." She talks as she pours. "You know, JD, I was thinking about what you asked me on Friday. About suicide and why I don't do it."

I sip, and it's black and sharp as razors, so bitter it feels like that poem about the thing eating its own heart. Stephen Crane.

I like it because it is bitter, and because it is my heart.

Poetic coffee.

I could say what I'm thinking to 1066 because she'd get it, but I don't. Feels like too much effort.

She sips from the cup on the thermos. "I don't think my prince is coming, JD."

"Jim," I croak. "Just call me Jim. JD is dead."

She keeps going, not skipping a beat. I love 1066. Love her like a brother.

"My prince isn't coming, Jim. And so I was thinking about why I should even waste another breath. And I think it's the little things."

Yeah, married parents, friends, someone to call when you're feeling blue, a nice anchor for a hangman's rope. The perfect suicide note. Little things.

She sips her coffee. "I like coffee a lot. And books. Good books. And I like it when I figure out something, a problem with my computer, or a hard math problem. And I like it when my uncle and I go driving in his hot rod."

Little things. But I remember her look from the other day, when she didn't tell me the whole truth and nothing but the truth, so help her God. Or Satan. Or whoever.

"Is that all?" I ask.

She's not going to come clean, but then she does.

"Dumb dreams," she says. "Maybe one day I'll win a Grammy."
What in the hell is that?

Before I can ask, she keeps going. "I know, I know, it's stupid, and it doesn't mean anything. It's a dumb dream, but maybe it keeps me going."

She turns around. Bells ring, classes start, teachers talk.

I forget all about 1066. I daydream that Marianne will sleep with me to save my life. The last bell rings, and I walk out into the halls. Well, after all the fantasies about Marianne, I have to adjust the crotch of my pants first, but I won't get graphic. At least I don't have to worry about running into Todd. He'll ignore me, and I'll ignore him, and never the twain shall meet.

Marianne finds me, standing dazed in the hallway, wondering what I'm going to do with the rest of the sixty years I have left on the planet. Or at least for the rest of the afternoon until I can sleep again. Writing a suicide note feels exactly like climbing Mount Everest, so I'll just sleep my life away.

"Jim, good to see you," Marianne says. "I just wanted you to know, we're all betting on you."

I have no idea she means that literally. Until later that week.

I smile and nod. "Thanks."

We have nothing more to say to each other. Nothing. We might as well be in two soundproof booths.

"Do you need a ride somewhere?" she asks after an eternity of awkward silence.

Risking a car ride of that same awkward silence, I say, "Yeah, I'm just going home. We can do it."

I wince, but she kind of laughs.

I'm eight days clean and suddenly everything I say is the wrong thing and can be taken a million different ways. I just want to get stoned. But I don't have anyone to get stoned with. And I don't want to be who I am when I'm stoned.

I follow her through the parking lot to her car. It's an early 90's Honda Civic. There's an electronic keyboard piano in the backseat, school papers, McDonald's wrappers, CD's and CD cases strewn about. Her iPod accoutrements fill up every nook and cranny.

Not what I expected.

"Sorry about the mess," she says.

We take off. My therapy hour is ticking, so I get to the point.

"I quit getting high last Sunday night. You'd think I'd just go back to getting loaded, right? I mean, if I'm so screwed up without partying, I might as well party. Right? But no, if life is inherently crappy, I want to know it, and then I want to choose to end it, and not limp along drugged out and stupid."

I look out the window so I don't have to look at her.

She kind of laughs, but not really. It sounds cold. "Now there is the most inspiring anti-drug message I've ever heard."

I laugh for both of us. That's funny. "No, I think I'm anything but. You look at me and say, what that youngster needs is a good, strong bong hit."

A pause.

"I thought about what you said," I say, feeling completely shy. "About the whole gift thing. But what do I have to give?"

She drives ferociously, changing lanes, shifting, downshifting. Manual transmission. Something I can't do. I watch her drive like a NASCAR racer on meth, and again, I can't get her to fit in my box where I put all good, Christian girls.

"I don't know what you're good at," she says in a blunt voice, bordering on frustration. "Maybe talk about not doing drugs, or staying in school, or I don't know. You're smart. You should be able to do something with your life."

"Maybe…"

We're turning onto my street. The ride has been a complete disaster. I open up my heart, and she's distant. The one person who can possibly save my life, and it feels like she's in Cleveland, visiting my mom.

She sighs. "I know. What are you doing tonight?"

"Committing suicide," I say automatically.

She shakes her head, no laugh. Maybe she's getting tired of my shtick. God knows I am.

"My youth group is going to a soup kitchen. I can pick you up in a couple of hours. What do you say?"

I look into her green eyes. Cat-green. And I look away, down at the pile of wires snarled around her stick shift.

"Come on, Jim, it will be fun."

"Fun." I have to laugh. "Fun at the soup kitchen. Fun with the bums. Fun with Doug. Sure. I'll go. I have nothing better to do."

"Except your whole suicide thing."

"It ain't much, but it's all I got." I give her a Cheshire grin as I disappear out her door. For a moment, I feel like me in the old days, with Todd and the gang, not caring about what anyone thinks.

"Hey, Jim." She's leaning down to look at me, and I lean inward, arms on the roof of her CVCC. I can see down her shirt. It's glorious down there. I look away because I don't want to be a sleaze.

However, she must have seen my eyes. And she didn't cover up. Instead, she might've smiled a little. My mind whirls. She's talking. "You have to wear a shirt and tie. Will that be a problem?"

"No, no problem." I need to go buy back some of my clothes from the Goodwill anyway. And underwear from Target. I'd call a Hazmat team to dispose of the ones I was wearing.

Marianne adds, "Doug's not going to be there, so you're safe."

"No, he's safe from me," I say.

She laughs, for real finally, and drives away. I feel better. I'd get Marianne. Her and her cleavage.

I'd get her, or die trying.

Well, or try dying, whatever the case may be.

CHAPTER EIGHTEEN

SECONDS IN THE SOUP KITCHEN

I spend the afternoon shopping. I find my old khakis, dress shirt, and tie at the Goodwill. Ten bucks for the whole thing. I buy another outfit, just in case I need it. With underwear from Target, I'm king of the world. Hurray. Clean underwear. Life is so stupid.

I tell my dad about going to the soup kitchen with Marianne and the Christians. It's the first time I've told him the truth in a long time, and I know he doubts me. In the back of his mind he thinks I'm going off to sin with Todd. I reassure him, Todd and I are over.

Later that night, I find myself riding in the back of Marianne's car with a girl-turned-mouse named Sheila. I want to call her Sheila E. but I think if I tried, she might shatter. Then I'd have to vacuum up what was left of her out of Marianne's car.

Riding shotgun is some huge guy named Carson. Grotesquely big Carson. Damn, they're growing Christians big these days. He was someone who should have been sent on the Crusades. He could have brought back Jerusalem on his shoulder.

I don't have anything against the Christians, or the Jews, or the Hindus, or the Muslims. I hate Buddhists, but that's only because they're watered-down Hindus. Just kidding.

What I hate is that unspoken, misguided superiority most Christians have. Like Doug. Doug was reaching down to help me out, and you know what? Keep on walking, Mr. Good Samaritan. I like the gutter, thank you.

Most of the Christians I've met think they have the answer, which is Jesus, and they think that I need the answer, which is Jesus. I need a lot of things. A way for the police to find my body and not my dad, a better suicide plan, any kind of suicide note that's not song lyrics, and sure, an answer to my life.

Why go on living? I need the answer to that question. Another good question? What is the purpose of my life?

If I'm looking for answers, start with your own questions first. Then we're even. Don't offer me the truth without first telling me when you've lied.

Something is up with Marianne. She's quiet, distant, and we are listening to some sort of new alternative thing on the radio. Poppy guitars and a guy singing all whiny. I would have preferred Gorge, or Type O Negative, or anything else.

The neighborhood gets worse. Then a little worse. Then bad. Then just broken.

We park, and I feel nervous. I'm strictly tagging along. I'm even following Sheila E. around. My tie strangles me, and I pull at the knot.

I'm a suburban kid, man. Denver ain't much of a city, but it's enough to freak me out a little.

Graffiti on brick is the going thing in east, east, east Denver. Nice red brick. Scrawling black paint. There are newspapers clogging up the gutters and a thick layer of dust on the windows. Filthy people shamble around like homeless zombies. Cars are either rusted out underneath or look abandoned. Surprise, one takes off, blowing

87

through a stop sign. Shocking. Where I come from, we stop at stop signs. Or at least pause.

Our little team of do-gooders step through a metal door that looks like something out of a Russian gulag. Inside it's noisy, and there are men on one side, women on the other. The XY's are dirty, doing the eating, and the XX's are clean, doing the cooking. I'm given the task of peeling potatoes, giving the gift of my hands to God.

No one talks to me, and I'm okay with that.

Carson, Sheila, and Marianne are doing other stuff, talking to other people they know, and we're all just cooking for Jesus.

I don't see the point, and I'm not feeling any better. You see, when you give me some boring task to do, the first thing I do is put my brain in high gear and crank up the volume. I chop up thoughts like bratwurst in a blender. Just when I think my *medulla oblongata* is about to liquefy and leak out my ears, the woman in charge, some beefy woman with huge wrists, says I can start wiping off tables.

It's all like a Taco Bell job I once had, except I'm not getting paid and the food isn't as good.

I enter the dining area. Mismatched chairs and rejected school tables. A cross on the wall hangs next to a picture of a hip, laughing Jesus you'd play basketball with if he were around today.

And men. Lots of unwashed men. And the smell. God. I mean, it seems to me once you smell like that, you are always going to smell like that no matter how hard you wash.

I feel something brush my arm like feathers, two feathers. I realize it's some old guy with teeth the color of dirt.

He mumbles something.

He's probably gripping me with all he's got. His thumb is completely stained nicotine yellow.

"Excuse me?" I say, not knowing what else to do.

"You think you're so cool."

What do you say to that? I say exactly what I think. "I'm not cool at all, man. I don't even know what I'm doing here."

His eyes aren't quite there. He's looking through me. I've seen Todd have that same expression on his face when he's completely gone.

"You think you're hot stuff, but you're not. You should just grow up."

The woman in charge comes up and eases the guy back down to his seat. "It's okay, Earl. It's all okay."

His gaze on me never wavers. I feel like I've turned neon because it seems like everyone is staring at me. I have to get out of there. I find Marianne in the kitchen, washing dishes.

"I'm taking off," I say.

"How are you going to get home?" she asks. I can see it. She's disappointed in me.

I lie and hope for once in my life I can lie well. "My dad's office is just around the corner. I called him and he can give me a ride."

"Okay." She casts her eyes down into the soapy, scummy water.

"We'll talk," I say.

She nods, and I go out the back, going around the vegetables they get from supermarkets. Donated vegetables they have to cut the rot off of so they can serve them. Pathetic. Horrible. Eating garbage that's just not in a trash can. And this is supposed to help me?

Out in the alleyway, I can breathe again. It smells like urine, but it's better than being inside.

I start jonesing. Hardcore. My guts are tied into triple hitches and I just want to smoke up my skull. Express elevator to stoned, going up.

I think about what I said to Marianne in the car, about me not wanting to run away from life. Well, screw it. If not getting stoned makes me this miserable, if not blazing up makes me want to kill myself, then everyone, and I mean everyone, will be happier if I just go back to the way things were.

What's my purpose, Inga? Getting lit and not giving a shit.

I can patch things up with Todd, my parents can stop worrying about me and start worrying about their divorce, and I can return to my regularly scheduled program. Posthaste.

Lucky me, I'm in East Denver, where Junky Pete gets his supply, where Todd comes when Gobble dries up. I can score here, take a bus back home, and get tore up from the floor up in the comfort of my own bedroom. It's the greatest plan ever devised by anyone ever.

I call my dad and say I'll be home late and not to wait up. Then I grab the first alleyway, looking to score, walking like I'm on my way to important business. Which I am. The back door to an apartment complex opens, and out pour four black guys, my age or a little older.

The timing is all wrong. They come out, and I nearly hit one of them. I'm not racist or anything, but I get scared. Four purple guys in that part of town would've freaked me out.

Or maybe it's because they're black. I don't know.

Sue me for being scared.

I know they are going to lay into me.

They do.

"Where you going?" one of them asks.

My life is over. Why should I be scared? I'm actively looking for a way to die. If I can't kill myself, maybe these guys can do the trick.

I find my care button and switch it off.

I stop walking and turn around.

All four of them stand a little straighter, and it's on.

The outlaw Josie Wales is back in town.

None of them have crazy eyes, but one of them has this cool look about him, like nothing can fry his bacon.

I decide I'll bait him first.

CHAPTER NINETEEN

YOU AND I WERE MEANT TO BE FRIENDS

"I was looking to buy either weed or a gun," I say, "but you nice gents probably wouldn't know anything about that."

The one with the cool eyes laughs. He has coffee-colored skin, a flat nose, and his hair is wild on his head, tied up with a blue cloth. His clothes are baggy, all the way down to his unlaced high tops. We have never met. I know we've never met, but there's something about him. It's like I've known him before in a past life or something.

"Nice gents, you say." He looks at my outfit, shirt, tie and slacks. "You going to a funeral?"

"Yeah, hopefully my own." I smile. Inside, I'm puking fear, but I give them a good front.

"We can help you with that," one of them says, a big guy with a deep voice. His skull is shaved down to the skin.

"Which part? The weed, the gun, or the funeral?"

Cool Eyes is looking at me. "Are you looking for trouble?"

"No, just death. But look, if you're just going to beat the bejesus out of me, then let's pass. If you're going to kill me, then we might talk. No witnesses except for the dumpsters. What do you say?"

Cool Eyes makes a sound of disbelief through his mouth, and then shakes his head. "That's racist. You think that just because we're black and you're white, that we would kill you. You ain't said the magic word."

"Please?" I ask, raising my eyebrow.

"No. Nigger," Cool Eyes says. "If you were serious, you would have called us that, and we'd take you out."

They all wait, but there's no tension in the air. Nothing. My tête-à-tête with Christian Doug had more sparks.

A smaller guy grins. "This is a waste of time, man. Let's go. We got stuff to do."

Cool Eyes doesn't move. "Are you going to say it?"

I shake my head. "No. I don't like the word. There's too much evil history in that word."

That catches Cool Eyes. "What do you mean?"

Everything I want to say is lame and bookish, but I don't care. "I studied a lot about this stuff in school. I had this really cool black teacher, and we watched *Roots*, and he talked about the 'N' word. Five hundred years of oppression and suffering are stuffed in that word, and it's not my place to say it."

They start laughing, one of them goes into the whole, Kunta Kinte – Toby bit. I figure they'll beat my ass for sure.

"I like you, Whitebread," Cool Eyes says. "What's your name?"

I should give him a fake name, but for some reason I don't. "Jim Dillenger," I say.

Cool Eyes throws his head back and does this little semi-laugh.

Big guy, baldy asks, "What is it Ray Ray? Why are you laughing?"

That was about as much emotion as I was going to get out of Ray Ray, Mr. Cool Eyes.

92

"You JD?" he asks.

And it's like my whole life has become one of those connect-the-number games. One to two to three until you have a picture of a Power Ranger, or in my case a suicidal teenager looking for weed.

Todd and I buy from Junky Pete, Junky Pete buys from Ray Ray. Or maybe it's Gobble, talking about crazy JD to his suppliers on the re-up.

Cool Eyes nods, smiles at his friends. "We have a celebrity out here in the ghetto. The Suicide King, all the way from Littleton. Can I have your autograph?"

"So you know Junky Pete?" I ask.

Ray Ray nods. "Don't everybody? Him and Gobble both talked about you. Some dope-fiend making a big deal about suicide. So you really are serious about dying. I bet you go east more on Colfax and walk around, someone'll jump you. Don't know if they'll kill you, but why you want to die anyway?"

Before I can even attempt to answer, one of his buddies, a tall, thin guy speaks up. "Ray, I gotta get to my sister's place. We gotta go."

"Sure, man. Yo, King, roll with us. I want to hear you out. I want your whole story."

The Suicide King. Where did that name come from? Ten bucks it was Todd. Oh, Lordy, Lordy, Lord. After years of avoiding Todd's wit, he's now aiming it at me. The universe sure isn't throwing me very many reasons to live.

I can't say no to the whole surreal encounter. I follow them to a white Escalade and get in. I'm a fish completely out of water. I'm a cod in a Cadillac.

But the Escalade smells like Todd's car. Cigarettes, a little weed, mixed with more cigarettes and weed, and underneath, stale cigarettes and weed. The thin guy lights up. He's riding shotgun. I'm stuck in the back with the big, bald guy and the smaller guy who keeps trying to inch away from me so we're not touching. I'm grateful for that. The big guy doesn't have such sensitivities.

We drop the thin guy off, and then go pick up other guys, and drop them off, and everyone keeps looking at me. I keep quiet, and my care button keeps getting turned on, and I keep sweating, but trying not to sweat. I'm thinking the homeless shelter was a better deal.

Ray Ray just keeps on smiling. He throws a thumb back at me and says, "He's a celebrity we're escorting around."

All the guys who get in and out keep saying, "Morgue is looking for you, Ray. And he's pissed this time. You know what he's like when he's pissed."

Ray Ray just shines them on. "I got Morgue. Get in or get out, whatever."

Morgue. They use his name to frighten ghosts out of haunted houses. Satan calls him Mr. Morgue, sir. What am I doing in a car with someone on the wrong side of Morgue?

Finally, around one in the morning, it's just Ray Ray and me. And on a school night? I'm very disappointed in me. Hopefully my dad slept through the night and I won't have to explain myself.

"I got weed, but I heard you quit," Ray Ray says. He points to the glove compartment. "It's in there. With papers."

The dope is just an arm reach and some finger play away.

I don't move. I don't say anything. He gets on Sixth Avenue going west, like he's going to drive me home.

"Why you want to die, King?" he asks.

I look over, and he looks at me, and he's serious. He wants to know.

Suddenly, I feel very white and very rich. Luxuriously rich. And suburban. And stupid.

"You don't want to know," I say back to him.

"Yo, King, I been driving you around all night because I want to know. How come you think your life is so bad?" He looks over at me. He's not going to take no for an answer. And I have the idea that Ray Ray generally gets what he wants, however young he is.

Words fall out of my mouth. Some even make sense. "My life ain't bad. It's just that I know what's going to happen. It's like I have a novel, and someone read me the end, and I know exactly how it's all going to unfold. So why bother? The story of my life is a crappy little book, and I'd rather not read it."

Ray Ray does his semi-laugh. "So you knew that you would hang out with a bunch of black guys all night long, and out of all the folks in Denver, you'd meet one that actually knew your sorry ass. Man, open that book. Tell me what the lottery numbers are going to be for next week."

"Not on the micro scale, but on the macro. Macro, like I see the big picture of my life."

"Micro like microscope. I ain't dumb, King."

He doesn't say it like he's going to pop the proverbial cap in my ass, but there's an edge to it.

Ray pushes me. "So tell me what you think is going to happen in your life."

I go through it all one more time with him. Job, wife, kids, Alzheimer's, death.

"And that's it," he says.

"That's it," I say with a sigh.

Ray smiles. "You think I'm driving you home."

"Yeah," I say, abruptly nervous. Isn't he driving me home?

"Maybe I'm driving you to kill you. Maybe I'm dropping you off for a booty call with a girl I know. Maybe I'm just going to drive us both to L.A. and pick up this massive supply coming in from Colombia. You don't know, now do you?"

He has me, but if he wants to argue, I'd be his huckleberry. I loves me a good debate. Debating with a drug-dealing gangster might be a little odd, but hey, I'm all about the odd. "Okay, Ray, so you beat the lovin' spoonfuls out of me, or hook me up with some strange, or we drive to L.A. It's all the same in the end. You can change the day-to-day, but the year-to-year is going to play out just like I know it will."

"Damn, if I thought like that, I would be the exact same as you."

He gets off on Rudyard and heads south. The mountains are wet shadows in the night.

"So what about your life?" I ask him.

"Get busted, go to prison, get out, and do it all over again. Just like my brother. Oh, and when I'm trying to go legit, I'll work at the worst jobs on the planet in between scoring, stealing and scamming. Like everyone I know. Oh, I forgot, I get to do that if I don't get shot in the head."

"But you don't think about stuff like that."

Ray shrugs. "Maybe I do sometimes. But then I forget about it. Maybe that's your problem. You just quit forgetting about it."

"Yeah," I say slowly. That's exactly what happened.

We drive in silence.

He's taking me home. Of course he's taking me home. And the next track of my life will start playing in pre-determined order. Before I know it, I'm laughing like a drunk clown. I have an idea, and it's so stupid I have to laugh about it.

"What?" Ray Ray asks.

"We switch books. Switch lives. I'll start driving around people, or drug dealing, or whatever. You can go to my high school, you graduate and you go to college and you live out my life." I'm still laughing at the whole idea.

"What's funny about that?" Ray asks.

And I then notice, he's not laughing.

I stop laughing, that uncomfortable-must-stop-laughing thing, and then I fall into the broke-care-button space. Who cares? What is he going to do, kill me? Ooh, so scared.

"Are you in school?"

"No." Ray answers.

"And you get to do whatever you want every day, right?"

"Yeah," Ray answers.

"And you make lots of money doing whatever, right?"

"Something like that," Ray answers.

"And you're going to give that up to do homework and deal with snooty, suburbanite, racist teenagers?"

Ray Ray doesn't say anything. I see him thinking.

When he talks, he changes the subject. "What if I didn't care about living no more? In the hood, you wouldn't last a day. Damn, like I'd go and steal money from Morgue. What if you had a million dollars? You saying you wouldn't want to keep on living? What about the book of your life then, King?"

There goes the boring-job-I-hated part of my life. I can travel, learn to play the guitar, true freedom. My dad can quit his job, and maybe my parents won't split up. Sure. Unlimited financial resources. I can go all Bono and change the world.

I smile. "You graduate and go to college, and I steal money from Morgue. How about that?"

"He'd cut you up if he heard you say that. You don't want to mess with Morgue. For real." The way he talks about Morgue cutting me up, he doesn't say it like it's a movie. He says it like prophecy.

I direct him to my house.

"Give me your number, King," he says. "We'll talk about your idea. I know how you could rip off Morgue, and maybe I'll mess up my own book and change things. Go to school, college, get out of the life."

Yeah, right.

I give him my number, and he smiles. "Similar numbers. Your number ends in 6886 and mine with 8668. This is crazy."

I again get that spooky feeling, like we are meant to be friends. He's right about one thing—I couldn't have seen this whole thing coming.

He waits until I get the door open before he drives off.

It's because he waits for me that I know he'll call, and he won't call to sell me drugs or a gun. He'll call about school.

About remembering not to forget.

A quick check. Inga got her mail. My dad forgot to get ours, so I take it inside. House is silent, and I know my dad didn't worry too much about me being out late. Not sure if that's a good thing, but it is what it is.

Before I go to bed, I set the coffee maker to go off so I can bring coffee to school. I'm sick and tired of being the recipient of charity. It's time I gave some charity back, just so I can be the one to feel morally superior.

Meeting Ray Ray is odd, but the next day at school, things take a dip into the downright surreal.

CHAPTER TWENTY

PAPARAZZI PHOTOGRAPHERS

Ray Ray was right. I'm a celebrity.

A group of freshman are pointing at me and whispering. Some sophomore steampunkers run up in a group, and all of them whip out their archaic phones to take pictures of me and my bewilderment.

Some random girl touches my arm and says, "I think you're going to make it. I'm betting on you to live."

She's vanilla blonde and small. Not my type.

"Thanks," I mutter.

Terrorist turned football player Brad Sutter points at me and laughs. His jock friends laugh. I keep walking. In class, everyone is pointing, looking, whispering, or trying not to point, look or whisper.

I slide into my desk behind 1066 and pop open the thermos of coffee I brought just for her.

"Here, Ten." I pour her a little of the Dillenger house blend.

She looks dubiously at the coffee. After a lifetime of playing out the darker bits of *Carrie*, I think she takes any act of kindness as a threat.

"What is this, Jim?" she asks.

"You like coffee. I'm planning on ending it all, so at least one of us should be happy."

She takes a sip. "Your odds are falling."

I lean close. "Ten, what is going on? Does everyone know?"

She nods. "Yeah, everyone. Brad Sutter has a betting pool. Your odds are falling. Losing all your friends kinda blew you away. I think you being nice to me isn't helping. But I knew once you and Marianne became friends, there was hope. Marianne is nice. She's in my band."

My mind reeled from all of it. Betting pool? Odds? What kind of band?

Too many questions to get my head around. I go with the band option. "What band? Like a marching band?"

"A rock and roll band. We do some early goth stuff. Nick Cave covers, now that Marianne can play piano for us. Lots of neo-punk as well."

"And you play…"

"Bass," she says and sips coffee. "I'm trying to convince them to learn *"YYZ"* by Rush. They think it's too classic rock-y. I get tired of playing all those fast, easy Green Day chords. The Nick Cave stuff is cool though."

Then I remembered, a Grammy.

"And you want to win a Grammy, which is like some music award?"

"Like I said, dumb dream, and Grammy's are inane anyway." More sips.

"Does Marianne have a boyfriend?" I ask. Not sure why I go with that question next. I guess my mind is trying to ignore the betting pool on my life.

1066 gets cagey. "Kind of."

"Kind of?"

1066 climbs into the metaphorical cage as in cagey and locks the door. "I can't talk about it. I promised. Don't ask."

Too much to think about. I go back to her burgeoning musical career. "What's the name of your band?"

"Penumbra," Ten says.

Then class starts, and I have to be quiet while the teacher starts up on Herman Hesse's *Siddhartha*. Yeah, rich prince, life is harsh, sickness and death, whatever. That is one book that has nothing to do with me.

After school, I take the long way home so I can buy back more clothes from the Goodwill. Embarrassing, but relatively cheap. I also need to stop and get some groceries. Even though my dad is home, he's so wrapped up in work and getting caught up on bills, he forgets we need to eat.

Gobble is out front of the King Soopers. Along with Ray Ray. Shivers shake my spine. It's too much of a coincidence.

I had to get up early for school, so I'm reeling from exhaustion. Ray Ray looks as fresh as flowers. Gobble is still vying for an ugly award.

"Hey, King," Ray Ray says, as if he's not at all surprised to see me.

"Hey, Ray." That's all I can manage. What's going on?

Gobble solves the mystery. "Ray was just re-upping me. We stopped to talk, and I was about to say what I thought of you."

"Of me?"

Gobble nods and his neck fat sways back and forth. It's hypnotizing.

"Yeah," he says. "JD is a good guy. I mean, he's in all the smart classes at school and he's gonna be somebody someday. And he says I should be careful of the cops 'cause I won't like prison. So he cares." Gobble turns bloodshot eyes on me. "You're not gonna kill yourself, right? That'd be stupid."

"Why's that, Gobble?" I ask. "Why is life so great?"

Gobble gives me the stoniest grin you've ever seen gracing the face of a street corner drug dealer. "Life is awesome, man. Like

Star Wars. You die, you don't get to watch *Star Wars* no more. And girls. Looking at girls and everything about girls. And I love that feeling when I got a pocketful of cash, and the work is done, and I get to hang out with my buddies and drink beers and get high. I got a sister with Down syndrome, man, and she's so freakin' happy. When I get all depressed sometimes, I look at her and I think, *If she can be happy, what's wrong with me?* So I get happy. Get happy, JD. I got some coke. That'll help."

Ray is watching me closely, to see what I'll say. I could tear Gobble's argument up like so much notebook paper. I don't. What's the point of that? "No, Gobble, I'm clean now. Nine days. And yeah, just gotta get happy. Easy. You okay, Ray?"

Ray shrugs. "Yeah. You really going to stay clean? You really in the smart classes?"

I get it. He's checking up on me, trying to figure out if I'm responsible enough to help him, or too much of a drug addict to be of any real use. "Can you not tell how brilliant I am?" I ask.

Ray laughs. "I can't tell yet. But I'm thinking you either might be the smartest guy I've ever met, or the dumbest. Depends on what you decide to do."

Is he talking about my suicide, or something else? I can't tell.

Again, I know he'll call me. I know, somehow, Ray's fate and mine are woven together like so much fettuccini.

Gobble is trying to catch the eye of a mom hurrying out, one of his morning post-carpool customers, no doubt. She keeps on walking.

So do I. I say goodbye to Gobble and Ray and head into the store, get some mac and cheese, some chicken wings, some apples and oranges because nutrition is important for the terminally suicidal.

I pay with the parental credit card. When I get outside, Ray is still there. Gobble is conducting a business transaction with an overweight guy holding a grocery bag filled with Cheeytos. Pretty sure Cheeytos keep half of the drug addicts in the world alive. I'd love to see that commercial.

"Need a ride home, King?" Ray asks.

"Sure."

We leave Gobble and I get back into the Escalade.

"I'm not stalking you," Ray says. "Just coincidence. You get that?"

"I get it," I say. "How are things with Morgue? You still on the run?"

He shrugs. With sunglasses on his face, I can't read him. Even without sunglasses, Ray emanates so much cool you could ice beer under his gaze.

When he speaks, his words are careful. "Look, what we talked about last night. It's crazy. I can't just go back to school. You know it's crazy, right? And you wouldn't want to mess around with Morgue and his people. He's for real, yo. Evil to the core."

It's like he's arguing with himself. Not sure how I can add anything. I just agree with him. "Yeah, crazy. Stuff like that doesn't happen. Trading lives? Whatever."

He doesn't laugh or smile or anything. He's thinking. Hard. "I mean, if I did go back to school, it would make sense to come out here. The schools are better than in the 'hood, and I wouldn't know anyone. It would make it easier. I'd be less tempted to get back into the game. But I left school when I was pretty young. I'd have a lot to catch up on. Besides, I'd have to live in the district, or whatever, right? No, it'd never work. My life is cool. Like Gobble said, I got my friends, and girls, and I like *Star Wars*."

Again, who am I to argue? What he's saying is right.

He pulls up in front of my house and we bump fists. "I still got your number, King. If I change my mind, I'll buzz ya. But seriously, man, don't kill yourself. That's messed up."

I see myself, clown-sized, in his sunglasses. I could shine him on. I could lie. I don't. I say exactly what's on my mind. "I have to find a reason to live, Ray. I need a purpose, and right now, all I'm seeing is a lot of meaningless nothing. Life is a joke. If I can learn to laugh at it, great. If not, I'm getting out. I can't live for *Star Wars*. Jar Jar Binks kind of ruined it for me."

He shakes his head. "Dang, man, you think way too much. Take it easy, King. Take it real easy."

Another fist bump. Again, Ray waits until I'm in my house before he drives off. I'm not sure if he's trying to talk himself into my plan of trading lives, or talk himself out of it.

The thought of living Ray's life scares the hell out of me, and yet, it's the perfect way to chase death down.

CHAPTER TWENTY-ONE

TIMES AROUND THE WORLD WITH INGALORA BLUTE

Still thinking of Ray, I can't get into my homework, but I do it anyway, listening to lots of Tool, Gorge, and Scattershot. Heavy metal turns normal studying into an epic event, and I highly recommend it.

My dad comes up from his office in the basement to check on me. He tells me he has to fly out the next day, but should be back on Friday night. Goody. Then he gets all serious. "Listen, Jim, I've been thinking about the big questions you've been asking. Maybe it's not so much about the answers, but more about the quality of the questions. Either way, I respect you for trying to find the meaning of life. The world would be a better place if more people thought about those things."

"Maybe you should ask some quality questions about Mom."

He kind of shrugs. "Yeah, I will be. Just take care of yourself. Please."

"Sure." Uh uh. Wasn't planning on it.

He leaves to pack, once again, while I go get the mail and check on Inga's mailbox. Uh huh, Inga's mailbox. Sounds kind of dirty, but it's anything but. I'm not about to go all *Harold and Maude*. Best. Suicide movie. Ever.

Outside, Inga is working on her front lawn, taking out the flowers along the path. She has one less plant to worry about after my whole kicking thing. Still felt bad about that. That's me, way too sensitive.

She's sitting on a little gardening stool with a cane next to her. She digs out one flower, throws it in a pile, wearily gets up, moves her stool, and sits down to work on another. It looks grueling. Why does she bother? If she can afford the house, she can afford a gardener.

I grab her mail and walk it over to her. "Got your mail, Inga," I say.

She smiles at me. "Why, James, I expected another note. But now a visit? I am a blessed woman indeed."

"Yeah, whatever," I say. I'm getting used to her smart-ass teasing. Though I'm not quite sure she's teasing.

I sit down in the grass. Schatzi comes bolting out of the bushes to lie on my lap, where he forces me to rub his belly. His eyes get narrow and his tongue lolls out. He's about in heaven.

"If only I was a dog," I say before I can stop myself. "Dogs are simple. They can be happy with just some food and good belly scratch."

"Who says people can't be so simple?" Inga asks. When I don't say anything, she laughs again. "So, what did you think of my note? Am I out of my mind?"

"No, I understand about the whole purpose thing. I just don't think I have any kind of purpose. Do you ever feel that way?"

She digs into the ground and throws another flower into the pile. "Of course. The secret is to alter your purpose when things change. Different seasons call for different flowers, if you will."

I don't ask why she planted flowers in the fall, but I have an idea. Instead I ask, "So what's your purpose now? Besides murdering those helpless plants."

"Oh, James, must you be so dramatic?" A pause as she moves her stool. I want to help her, but it's obvious she's having another one of her odd elderly adventures. "For a long time, I worked as a surgeon all over the world. Do you know Doctors Without Borders? I was an inaugural member. I have been up to my elbows in blood on every single continent. Now that was a purpose."

I remembered how against hip surgery she was, and I remind her.

She laughs. "I don't want surgery because I know all the things that can go wrong. Doctors make the very worst patients."

I'm trying to imagine what kind of nightmare third world countries she's been in, when she talks more.

"I'm sure you don't want to hear my life's history. It is not a video game. Not at all. But I will give you the choicest bits. I couldn't have children. I never married. I've spent a great deal of time in asylums when I wasn't working in hospitals all over Europe. If you had a light bulb, I would show the results of too much electro-shock therapy."

I try not to let my mouth drop open. I fail.

More laughter from my girl Inga. "As I told you, I know about the darkness. The medication I'm on is very effective, but I still need a purpose. I volunteer at free clinics downtown, I work with the poor, I even sing in the church choir, though I mouth the words as much as I sing." She puts a finger to her lips. "Shush about that last part. I'm doing it as a favor for a friend."

"Really, electro-shock therapy?" I ask.

"Yes, but you knew I was kidding about the light bulb, right?"

I nod. "Yeah. My school counselor says I should try anti-depressants. Seems like a cop-out to me."

She tsk tsks me. "James, you are a Neanderthal. If you had diabetes, you wouldn't think insulin was, what did you call it, a copping out? Am I wrong?"

"No, but that seems different."

She shrugs. "Of course. But perhaps you are trying to fix a broken mind with a broken mind. I don't know, and it is none of my business. As one who has been diagnosed with severe mental illnesses, I take my medication and I'm grateful to God for it. I'm sure you don't believe in anything as mundane as God."

"Don't go there." I have to warn her. We're treading on dangerous ground.

"And why not? Either you believe or you don't. Or are you an agnostic? Tell me you aren't. I find them wishy-washy. Commit fully to either theism or atheism, but do not sit on the fence like the arrogant or the unimaginative."

"Sorry, Inga, but until I have proof, I'm not going to believe in anything. Color me agnostic."

"How very disappointing," she grumbles, but is still smiling. She's not taking any of this seriously, or at least I don't think she is.

"Yeah," I say, "I know. I got into an argument with Christians the other night. I'm assuming you're Christian."

"Yes, that's a good idea. Let's put a label on something that is unknowable. Very smart." She winks at me. "I attend an Episcopalian church and it soothes me. I enjoy the stories. You do know we are all Jesus, don't you?"

"How does that work?"

"Am I boring you?" She's grinning like a leprechaun, tipsy on Guinness.

"No. I gotta hear this. How am I Jesus?"

She's done with the flowers. She pats her leg and Schatzi runs over to her. "The divine becoming human is an ancient story. Many different versions, but the same idea. Christianity is just the latest flavor." She gives Schatzi a scratch under the chin. "We are born to be gods, James, and yet we are still so imperfect and human. We are Jesus, human and divine, sinner and saint, heaven and hell. All mixed together. When everything fails me, James, I do what the master did. I look for feet to wash. I pray to be a servant."

Marianne's argument again. Like an MP3 on repeat.

Inga falls silent, and I know she's done talking. She'll make some smart-ass comment and go inside. Maybe prepare for choir practice, or leave to heal a leper.

I'm in awe of her. You know why most kids don't like old people? Because most old people are boring as hell. Not Inga.

"And now, James, we can be done. Or would you like to tell me your story? For in the end, all we have is our story."

I don't want to say a thing. After all she's seen and experienced, whatever I say is going to come out lame.

Yeah, but I talk anyway. Spill the beans. "I met a guy from downtown. We're thinking about trading lives. But people don't do that, right? That's crazy, him coming to my school, and me doing what he does. I think he might be serious though. As for me, I have to do something. I have to figure out life, or I'm not going to make it. Everyone is calling me the Suicide King. I'm stupidly famous, all of a sudden, because I can't find a reason to go on living."

She doesn't say anything for a long time. She pets Schatzi in silence. For a minute I think she's pulled a Grandpa Simpson and fallen asleep.

"It's not my place to say a word," she says, "but if I had killed myself at seventeen, I would've been killing a stranger. It took decades for me to understand myself, and maybe that is what life is. Discovering one's self."

She's watching me carefully, gauging my reaction.

I stay stone-faced, but I have to look away. She's like the Buddha, or whatever, and I'm so out of my league.

Inga's voice changes a bit, gets a little less light. "The last thing in the world you need is the advice of an old woman. But if you would allow me to make a suggestion, I would do things that don't make sense. Follow your heart. Pray to your nothing god, for a nothing god is just as powerful as an everything god. Consider medication, though I know you resist the idea, and so you choose your pain as I chose my pain. Freedom can be such a terrible thing."

She stands up. "My door is always open to you. Or leave notes in my mailbox, which is so very Dickens. I would help you, if you'd allow it, but that would take an incredibly open mind on your part. How worried should I be, James?"

Still on the grass, I shrug. I don't know. I really don't know.

Inga picks up her stool, then leans on her cane. "The hardest thing I have ever done in my life is to ask for help. In the end, however, I copped out, and I daresay the world is better for it."

"Thanks, Inga. If I need you, I'll come by."

"Do it soon," she says with a smile. "I have scheduled surgery despite my fears. My hip, it seems, has convinced me to be open-minded. Once again I've asked for help."

"When is the surgery?" I ask.

"Why do you want to know? Do you want to bring me flowers?. Oh, James, how romantic."

I blush.

She laughs and goes inside. But not before blowing me a kiss.

I do more homework, but I can't quite get Inga and her life story out of my mind. From mental institutions to international surgery, and here she is, at the very end of her life, still planting flowers even though it all ends in death.

I can't match that. Not even close.

But the next day, I find a purpose. Kind of.

CHAPTER TWENTY-TWO

WITH MY PAL THE PRINCIPAL

My dad's already gone when I get up. He left me a quick note.

Dear Jim,
    The biggest question I have about the divorce is how you are going to handle it. Other questions? What do I want out of life? What do I want from a partner? Can years of trouble disappear? You know how your mother is. She used to be so different. Losing her father changed things. For all of us. Know that whatever happens, we both love you.
Love,
Your Dad

I have to sigh. Yeah, I know how my mom is.
I'm getting ready when I realize my suicide idea is a week old. Happy birthday, Suicide, now blow out your candles. I put on my

soup kitchen clothes, sans tie, from Monday. Gotta make another trip to the Goodwill, my own personal closet. Gotta get a suicide note then bust on over to Todd's to use one of his firearms, so I don't have to keep buying back my old clothes. My twisted to-do list is calling.

Problem is, killing myself is feeling harder than ever, now that Inga's voice is rolling around in my head. I also have Ray Ray to consider, and Marianne, sweet Marianne, is waiting for my scalding-hot kiss. And there's my dad and his questions.

I'm pondering all this in my last class of the day, physics, hurray, when I get the official note summoning me. I expect counselor. Instead, it's principal. Not spelled principle, because the principal is your pal. I go, grateful to be missing physics.

The hallway has that eerie class-is-in-session feel to it. Like veins without blood. I'm shuffling toward my pal's office when Annie pops out of the girl's bathroom.

Annie. Dreamboat Annie. Talk about too classic rock-y.

She stops me. "It's bullshit, JD."

She has that mean-stoner-chick thing going. Eyes blazing, blonde hair standing on end. Cigarettes, perfume and leather. I want to crawl into that smell and die.

"Look, I'm sorry. I didn't mean for this thing to get out—"

She cuts me off. "My brother killed himself. You know what that does to people? You know what that did to me and my parents?"

"Annie, it's not what you think. I'm not serious."

Her angry eyes flood with tears. "I don't care. You talking about it makes other people think it's okay."

"Like what other people?"

She stops and explores her brain for something, to see if it's okay to say. "Like Todd maybe. He's started talking about suicide. Said maybe you were right. See what you did? I used to think you were nice. But now I know you're just a selfish asshole."

She knows she can stop there, so she takes off and storms down the hall, sobbing.

I feel gutted, then I find the cold place in my heart and settle in. Poor Annie. It's messed up, but then, life is a shit sandwich and every day another bite. What did she expect?

What about your dad, Jim? How would he handle all this?

No, can't think about that, hello cold place, glad to see me?

My cell phone starts vibrating in my pocket.

Ray Ray is on the phone. "Okay, King, I have to know how serious you are about helping me get into school. I gotta know right now."

I can't answer him right then, too shocked and overwhelmed. At least I have a new official nickname, King, as in Suicide King. Thank you, R2B2. Ray Ray Too Black. Never mind. Don't know why I have this thing with people's names, but I have embraced it.

"R2, what's new?" I ask. Annie broke me and I was back in my never-care-again configuration.

"So I do your thing, King. School and college. That changes my book. What about your book?"

I lean against the wall. The principal will have to wait. What's he going to do? Expel me for being suicidal?

"That's the thing, R2. My book can't change. Written in stone. Never to be changed." I know Inga would disagree, but then she's Ingalora Blute, and I'm just Jim Dillenger.

"What's this R2 you calling me?" Ray asks.

I briefly explain square roots and square numbers and why *Alien 3* was Alien cubed. He gets it.

"You have a car, King?" he asks.

"Not really, but I could swing something, maybe. Why?"

"I go to school. You come and drive for Morgue. He's going to need someone, and you knowing the suburbs is going to give you an in. How about that for changing your book?"

"You're serious?"

"I'll call you tonight. What time do you get out of class?"

I laugh too loud, and it echoes down the hall. A pissed off teacher gives me a dirty look and closes her door. "I'm in class right now, R2. On my way to the principal's office."

His voice changes. "Don't mess up and get kicked out of school, King. I'm liking this idea more and more. Beats dyin', man."

He's serious. Lordy, how am I going to get him into my school? How much did he know? Did he drop out when he was like five? Could he keep up? *Now you've gone and done it, Jimmy. What a fine mess you've gotten yourself into.*

I hang up, and who do you think is sitting in the principal's office? Not just the principal and Mrs. Farmer the counselor, but Brad Bet-You're-Going-To-Die Sutter. It's a grand little board meeting.

Mr. Gelb, Principal and CEO of Coyote Ridge High School, motions to a chair. "Sit down, Jim. We have to talk." Mr. Gelb is a thin little man, thin-necked, thin-souled, thin-skinned. Thin.

Still reeling from Ray's bit of news, I'm not up for another mental scrubbing. My brain is gone. Bye, bye. Out to lunch. Take the rest of the day off, Dillenger. You deserve it. I am beyond all reach.

I manage to sit down. Just.

Everyone is looking at me.

"Who started it?" Mr. Gelb asks.

"What?" I grunt. Teenager one syllable for leave me alone.

Mr. Gelb hisses a sigh. "I am not messing around here. Suicide must be taken seriously."

You could say it's a life or death matter. I think it, but I don't say it. I'm still mystified.

Sutter finally talks. "He's suicidal, sir. I'm fine."

Ooh, sir. Please.

Mr. Gelb gives him a red-faced, angry look. "Are you, Brad? Aren't you betting that...that..."

Good God, he's forgotten my name.

"Jim," whispers Mrs. Farmer.

"Aren't you betting that Jim is going to kill himself?" Mr. Gelb asks.

Sutter feigns innocence. Complete innocence. "No, sir. I talked with Jim just the other day and tried to convince him to live. I'm bucking for him, sir."

I can't help myself. I mouth "bucking," trying to figure out what the etymology for the word might be. I'm guessing some sort of cowboy reference. But bucking, who uses that word?

"What's that, Jim?" Mr. Gelb hits me with a flash of anger.

"Nothing," I say. Hmm, so far I've said, "what" and "nothing". I'm doing well.

Mr. Gelb sighs, and I think I hear his skin crackle. "This has got to stop. No more suicide. No more bets."

That helps me. I'll straighten right up after such an authoritative statement.

Mr. Gelb focuses in on Sutter. "I'm sure Coach Ramirez will agree with me, but if I find out you are running any sort of betting at this school, I'll see you riding the bench."

Sutter hangs his head and nods. Ah, hit the jock where he lives.

Mr. Gelb dismisses him.

I'm left alone. I'm the real problem anyway.

Mr. Gelb then puts on his counselor's cap. "Now, Jim. What's the problem? I see your grades are good. Maybe you don't hang around with the best of the bunch, but I think you're a bright young man. What can we do to help you?"

I shrug. Okay, let's keep score. I said, "what," "nothing," and now a shrug.

Mr. Gelb doesn't say anything. Just looks at me.

Another shrug from our boy Jimmy. Something is creeping around in my head, but I don't know how to get from A to B with it.

"Jim, if you are doing this for attention, you got it. Even the faculty knows about our Suicide King. If you need professional help, we can arrange that. Even maybe make your classes easier. Come on, it can't be that bad."

I'm trying to formulate a plan, but what he says makes me insane with rage. It can't be that bad. What does he know? I could be selling my ass on Colfax for cheeseburgers. How does he know my life isn't a nightmare? He can't even remember my name.

Then it hits me. They can't stop me from killing myself. He is pleading with me, albeit poorly, not to off myself on his watch because then 9 News would come and talk to him, and he would have to admit he messed up big time. I hold all the cards.

What I need from him isn't so bad…it's actually noble. Sure. My purpose. Thank you, Inga.

I hesitate because I know my voice is going to crack like ice on a warming pond. I can't sound weak. I have to keep in control. "Look, I'm not doing well. You don't know my life isn't bad, so don't go there. This is what I need from you. I have a friend who is trying to straighten out his life. I need you to admit him to the school even though he's outside of the district. Like way outside. You do that, and I promise I won't…I won't do anything stupid."

Yeah, don't accept the promise of anyone suicidal. If they go back on their word, they won't be around to yell at. Don't lend them money either.

Mr. Gelb leans back. I feel like I'm playing at some Ultimate Poker Championship, and I just bet high, real high.

He's looking at his cards. He's trying to see if I'm bluffing. He's weighing the odds. Fourth street. The river. I might be holding the ace of spades after all. Or the Suicide King, the king of hearts.

"I can't do that," he says. He's not buying me at all.

I look him in the eye. "I can do it, sir. I will do it. And I'll be sure to mention you personally in my note."

Both Mrs. Farmer and the principal freeze. I went all in. Either I will get Ray Ray into the school, or I'll soon be wearing a jacket that zips up in the back. Electro-shock therapy for Jimmy. Iron Maiden album covers come to mind.

I've watched enough poker to know that I have to shut up, drop all emotion from my face, and wait.

I can feel the seconds falling like atomic bombs.

Mr. Gelb smiles a wispy little smile. "This is ridiculous."

I don't move. Not a flinch. Nothing.

Mrs. Farmer caves right in. "I know someone at the district. I think we should do it. Marianne Hartley believes in him. She thinks he's on the right track. And he's not hanging out with the bridge problem people anymore."

They had gone CIA on my butt all right. I wouldn't be surprised if they knew what I had for breakfast.

But Mrs. Farmer blew it. One thing I learned from my mom, never bargain out in the open. Once you start talking price in front of the client, they win.

Mr. Gelb knows the same thing. He turns real slow to look at Mrs. Farmer, and gives her an unbelieving look. Then he's back looking at me. "One problem out of you or your friend, and I swear, I'll do everything I can to…"

His voice fades away because he knows he's powerless. What can he do? Expel Ray and punish me? What if I'm not breathing anymore? Hard to punish the dead.

And I have Marianne Hartley to thank. She went to the wall for me. I would have to kiss her to thank her. Or Ray would.

I look at Mrs. Farmer. "Okay, the final part of the deal. You have your forms. You have my promise. So no sending me off to Emergency Psychiatric Services for a 72 hour hold. Are you good with that?"

She nods. "It looks like you've found a reason to live."

I want to shrug what she said away, but I don't. "I think I have. I really do. Thanks so much for helping.""No one needs to know about what we talked about today, Jim." The principal has folded. I'm raking in my chips.

Too bad Sutter doesn't want to share in my victory.

I'm out of the office, walking back down the hall, a little shaky, still a little baffled that all this is happening to simple Jimmy Dillenger, and then Sutter grabs me and throws me up against the wall, right against a school spirit poster. I can feel the glitter flutter down on my cheeks. It probably makes me look like a prom queen.

Sutter is not impressed.

"I got five hundred bucks that says you kill yourself, Dillenger. You ain't gonna let me down now, are you?"

CHAPTER TWENTY-THREE

TORN UP BOOKS

"You already own John Madden's Football for your Xbox, Brad. What would you need any more money for?" I ask. The hallway is as empty as Sutter's heart and my soul.

He ignores my wit.

"Let me give you a piece of advice, freak."

This I gotta hear. I am all ears.

"You want to die, just keep on with Marianne. She will feed your heart to you, gift-wrapped." He's glaring in my face, but I can't help but smile at what he said. Nice turn of phrase, though a bit of a mixed metaphor. Feed me something gift-wrapped. Not really workable, but a nice try.

"Marianne Hartley?" I ask. "Are we talking about the same Marianne?"

He nods. "When I heard about you and her, I really went all in.

You don't know what you are in for. She is going to tear you up, and in your present state, that works out just fine for me."

"Marianne?" I repeat. Could my day, could my entire life get any more whacked out? Just a word out there to our listening audience. You want to trip like I do, you want the best high around, just quit smoking dope and getting drunk. Life becomes inexplicably weird right away. "Marianne?"

Sutter lets me down and backs away. He smiles at me like a shark staring down chum. "Can't have people seeing us together. Might hurt my spread. But I give you until Halloween. If you're not dead by Halloween, I might have to get busy on your ass. But make it look like an accident of course."

"Why, Brad, how psycho of you. I never would have guessed."

He taps his head twice, hard, and I'm not sure what that means, but he hits himself hard enough for me to think that he might be unhinged enough to do anything. Brad Sutter killing me. That would be funny.

Last bell rings and students flood the hallway.

I have to find 1066. I have to know more about Marianne.

I start running, but then everyone, and I mean everyone, looks at me.

I slow down. Back at my Physics class, 1066 is nowhere to be found. I grab my stuff and realize I don't know where she lives, how she gets to school, nothing. Marianne is not in her room, and I'm glad. Suddenly, her moods, her drowning, seem sinister.

At the fight, I saw Marianne and Sutter had a history together, but now I need to know what kind of history.

But who was I kidding? Marianne and Sutter? No way. Sutter hung out with the gloriously beautiful, popular, crowd. Girls who are one uncle away from royalty. What would he be doing with plain old Marianne?

I'm not running, but I'm walking fast. Some wise guy yells out, "Lemming alert. Lemming alert."

I give him the finger.

I see a crowd in black heading toward the bridge. Todd catches my eye, and then raises a finger to his temple, like he's shooting himself with one of his many guns.

He turns away before I can do anything.

I'm in the parking lot, looking around trying to catch my breath. Did you know smoking a joint is like smoking five packs of unfiltered Camels? Or something like that. My lungs are cackling at me as if to say, "It's payback time, you unhealthy bastard."

Cars are all leaving in a long line, and I don't see Marianne's Honda, and I don't see 1066 anywhere. It will have to wait.

On the way home, I stop by the barking dog, and he just looks at me. Doesn't bark a bit. If only he had kept his yapper shut the other day, my whole life might be different. I thought he always barked at me. Maybe I was wrong.

I see the construction worker guy studying me from behind a curtain. Funny, all this power I suddenly got just because I had given up on living.

I try to shut my head off for the rest of the walk home, but I fail miserably.

Ray Ray is sitting in his white Escalade in front of my house. Before I can tell him the good news, he jerks his head for me to get in. "I'm about to rip up your book, King. Ain't nothing gonna be the same after today."

CHAPTER TWENTY-FOUR

IN THROUGH THE OUT DOOR
WITH DEVILS, DEALERS AND CLEAVERS

It's pretty much reverse commute. We're heading downtown and everyone is dispersing back into the suburbs.

Ray is quiet. We're listening to some old school on the stereo—Marvin Gaye, the Temptations—not the hardcore rap I would've thought.

"I talked to the principal today," I tell him. "He's gonna talk to people at the district to get you in. I mean, if this is really what you want."

He shrugs.

Not sure what to make of it.

"He said they're going to need your transcripts. When was the last time you were in school?" I ask.

"Eighth grade," he says. Then he starts talking, but not about school. "You're going to meet Morgue. I got it set up. Don't mention my name. He's looking for me, and I don't want you to say nothing. I'm betting once he finds someone to drive for him, he'll forget about me. Just be cool. And remember, Morgue don't care whether you live or die."

"That makes two of us," I say, acting tough.

"You don't know nothing, but you will," Ray says under his breath. Like he's deep into his own soliloquy.

"Are you really going to go back to school?" I ask.

"Only if you drive for Morgue. We'll see which one of us lasts longer."

Ah, he's questioning my suicidal depravity. Well, we can't have that. I sit and stew in my own indignation. He doesn't take me to East Colfax, but to the lower downtown area where the lofts are expensive and the beer is pub-brewed. We park on the street next to some swank restaurant with a thin little blue neon sign turned off. The sign is so stylized I can't tell what the name of the restaurant is.

Ray doesn't move to get out, but motions for me to go inside. "They're waiting for you inside. Good luck."

I'm about to get out when he stops me. "This is crazy, King. You know that. Me going back to school. You doing this. This kind of thing just don't happen."

I look at him, and I get that sense again, like we've known each other for years. I see that he's either really nervous about me meeting Morgue, or he's real nervous about going back to school. Maybe both.

I try and reassure him. "A friend told me I should do stuff that's crazy. It'll be all right."

"This ain't just crazy," he says. "This is dangerous and stupid, but you wanted your life to change. This'll do it. Change both of our lives." He points to a parking garage. "Call me when you're done, and I'll go up to the top floor and meet you there."

He drives off, and I go through the doors into what I think is the restaurant, but it turns out to be just a little entryway.

Inside, it's dark. Like walking into your own shadow.

The door to the restaurant opens, but it's as dark in there as it is in the entryway. I hear a voice, a shuffle. "This is him. Let's take him over."

The voice is deep, with an African-American accent. Another voice answers. Just as deep. "Yeah, let's go."

I feel arms grab me. A blindfold is slipped over my head and I'm handcuffed before I know what's going on. I'm sweating like gym class in August. I haven't eaten anything, and I'm glad. Good chance I'd throw it all up. Both men are wearing their fair share of aftershave. Their share and mine.

I'm hustled out where I smell fresh air for a minute, and then I'm put in a car and back into their smell. The book of my life has turned into a gangster movie. And we all know how gangster movies end. Drugged-out psychopaths with automatic weapons screaming, "Say hello to my little friend!"

The car stops. We've driven maybe a half a dozen blocks. They hustle me into a place where everything echoes. Some kind of door opens and closes around me. I sense an elevator going up, doors open, I'm pushed through, and then the blindfold is taken off, but the handcuffs are left on.

I'm trying to blink sight back into my eyes when I see the elevator close. And then I hear his voice.

It's solid. Like oak. He sounds smarter than I could ever hope to be. "So you are the Suicide King. It is a pleasure to meet you."

I'm spellbound he knows who I am. So surreal. I walk across the bare concrete floor of an empty warehouse. The windows are way up high, and the light they give is spectral.

In the middle of the warehouse sits a desk, a beautiful desk. Dark marble and darker wood. Two green lights shine down on a leather blotter. On it is an iPad and a meat cleaver.

The man behind the desk is big, athletic, with lifeless brown eyes and thick African features. He has short hair and only lines for a beard. He wears a black suit, black shirt, black tie. On his hands are sleek, shiny leather gloves. Black. This has to be Morgue.

I'm so far out of my normal reality, I feel like I'm about to wet myself.

From his leather chair, he points to a cheap, aluminum folding chair in front of his desk. No accident it's some Wal-Mart chair.

He wants the peons to feel their cheap seat while he's sitting on padded leather.

And it strikes me, the principal at my school has the same lights on his desk. Ironic.

I walk over and sit down in the chair. I have to sit to the side because my hands are still handcuffed behind me.

"Ray dropped you off," he says. "I have some objections with Ray at present. But I'm not worried. He thinks he is running. I am simply not closing my fist." A long pause. "Word has it that he is going back to school to better himself. I wish him luck with that."

My stomach feels like it's wrapped around my spine. I'm trembling like a guinea pig.

He looks at me, and I feel like I've been slapped. "Do you know why I like my office in such a large space?"

I shake my head slowly. I'm afraid any sort of quick motion might make him leap for my throat like a pit bull. My eyes keep going from his serene face to the cleaver on his desk. There is nothing behind his eyes. They are dark mirrors.

"We wind up in a small box in the end, Mr. Dillenger. The rich, the poor, the wise, and the damned all die and are boxed up. Are you truly weary of your life, Mr. Dillenger?"

I can't do my normal teenager shtick. No one-syllable replies. No shrugs. Morgue won't stand for that.

"I don't think there's really any meaning in life," I say and my voice trips over every crack and cranny of the sentence.

He laughs and it is rich and powerful. It reminds me of the wood on his desk, forever strong.

"There is no meaning, Jim. There are only those who take what they want, and those that give up everything they have. I had trouble with meaning when I was your age. I grew angry. I shook my fist at the broad firmament and told the empty sky that I would rage against this world with every fiber of my being. I didn't care if I lived or died. I was my own suicide. I was my own king. There is power in that. Doubtless, you have seen the power of stepping outside of your life."

The way he's talking, it's as if he knows everything there is to know about me. Like he has written the book of my life. How can he know anything about me, some suburban white kid?

He goes on. "It is the death of pride and ego that set us free. That's why the suicidal feel like they are powerful. They have died to themselves and can now truly live. Yet. Yet they are misguided because life is precious. Too precious to take lightly."

I'm looking away, and somehow he grabs my eyes with his.

"Are you sure you want to drive for me, Mr. Dillenger?"

Before I can answer, he smiles a soulless smile under those soulless eyes. "Dillenger is such a good gangster's name. I watched many of those films growing up."

Truth be told, I don't want to drive for him. I don't want to spend five more minutes around him. He's off. He and the cleaver on his desk are made from the same stuff and have the same purpose.

I want to drop back into my old, who-cares-life-is-crap attitude around him, joking about his name, that whole thing. I can't imagine doing that around him. He's handcuffed my heart to my ass, and I can barely talk.

I want to say, N*o, I'm not gonna drive for you, Mr. Psycho*, but then I think about Ray. Ray is probably as terrified as I am, about going back to school at a lily-white high school in the suburbs. Ray wants his life to change, but he has Morgue breathing down his neck. If I took over driving, it would allow Ray a chance to change his life. I've found my purpose. Lucky me.

"Are you sure you want to drive for me, Mr. Dillenger?" he asks again.

I nod. I can't talk. *Sure, I'll drive for you, you drug dealing, snake-eyed sociopath. Why not?*

"My father was a butcher," he says. "He left me his cleaver. I keep it very sharp. I use the cleaver to cut off the hands of thieves who steal from me. I cut off their hands, and I cut off their feet, and I throw the thieves into the sewer. You will not see me again, Mr. Dillenger. You will work for me through various agents, but you will not see me again unless you are to be rewarded or punished. I am interested in you, Mr. Dillenger. I am interested in the power of your suicide. I would recommend you use that power to devour the world."

He gingerly presses the screen of the iPad, and I hear the elevator open up.

He's done with me.

The blindfold is back on, no words are exchanged, and I am taken back down the elevator, into the car, into the restaurant, and this time, when the blindfold is removed, the restaurant is lit dimly and there are people eating.

They take me out back, and by the dumpsters, there is a short black man with a razor-thin moustache and gold teeth. He's wearing a screaming yellow jumpsuit.

The yellow man hands me an Eagle Creek backpack. "So, cracker, you gotta take this backpack to this address here." He flings a business card at me with an address written on the back. "You get caught, you don't know nothing. Right? You don't jack this up, we'll give you another job. You do jack this up, and I'll tell Morgue that he not only should cap your funky white ass, but also little ol' Ray Ray. Schoolboy Ray. Punk-ass bitches, the both of you."

Call me racist, but Mr. Yellow is totally what I was expecting when I thought I'd be working for gangsters. Not Morgue and his clear, deep voice and very educated diction.

I shoulder the backpack and walk on weak legs over to the parking garage.

I feel cold, empty, numb, hung-over from the fear and adrenaline. Talking with Morgue, I hadn't been able to say a word. I'd been a scared little white boy. Here I am, the Suicide King, but when it came right down to it, I shivered in front of death and prayed for life.

It pisses me off.

I will steal from Morgue, and I will steal big. I'll let my actions speak louder than my words. And either I'll get caught and killed, or I'll be rich and away.

The determination sets up in my guts like concrete.

I am not going to be a scared little boy ever again. Never. Death is better than that.

CHAPTER TWENTY-FIVE

WHERE THE CITY MOUSE
AND SUBURBAN MOUSE COMPARE NOTES

Ray drives up, and I get inside, with the backpack between my knees.

"Can you drop me off at the airport?" I ask.

He nods. He looks gray and frightened, like he's been talking to Morgue. No more Mr. Cool Eyes. Silently, he pulls back onto the street and heads for the highway.

"I'll pick up my dad's car so you don't have to drive me home," I say. I didn't want Ray involved anymore. I'm Morgue's delivery boy now. And I'm going to make him proud until I screw him over. Which brings me to my next question. "So, how am I going to rip off Morgue?"

He turns and looks at me. "I'm sorry, King. I messed up. I never should have made you go through that. He did his whole blindfold, cleaver thing, huh? Said he'd throw you in the sewer? He's for real. I shouldn't have brought you in. I'm sorry."

I try and smile, but I don't feel like smiling. "No, it's okay. I mean, he has to do that. He has to prove he's a badass."

"Damn," Ray Ray sighs, "he ain't got to prove nothin'. Everyone knows he's a badass. I'm still sorry. I guess, you pissed me off, King."

"How's that?" I ask.

"You think your life is so bad, and you think what I got is so easy. You don't know a thing, and I hate that. I hate, what they call it, when you're all innocent and stupid and don't know a goddamn thing."

"Naïve," I say. I feel my guts shift. Ray's right. That's what I was, but five minutes with Morgue had helped with my condition.

"Anyway, I'm sorry."

I'm hating the way I feel, so I repeat my question. "How am I going to rip off Morgue?"

"Halloween drop at the restaurant. You go through a back window and right into his money. Hopefully, K-Zee or one of his guys ain't around when you do it. Make off with a couple of million probably. You get caught, you get the cleaver. But, King, listen, it ain't worth it. Morgue'll hunt you down."

"K-Zee is our guy in yellow, right? Like a bad impersonation of Flavor Flav?"

Ray chuckles. "Yeah. That's him."

I nod, thinking about Halloween. It seems like a long time away.

"I called my old middle school," Ray says. "They're going to send over my transcripts to Coyote Ridge High School. It's really gonna happen. I'm going back to school. Damn."

He swallows hard. He's as scared as I am. Why are we doing this again?

Ray stops outside the airport's parking lot. I get out, and he frowns. "Yo, King, don't think you gotta do this thing with Morgue to be cool, or whatever. We can get you out of it. Maybe you should hang on to your naiveté a little longer."

I ignore the whole cool thing. "Naiveté, not bad. How do you know that word?"

"A lot you don't know about me, King."

"We'll talk," I say.

And Ray being Ray, he waits in the white Escalade until I drive out in my dad's Lexus, paying the guy for the parking. My dad keeps a spare key hidden in a magnetic holder under the wheel well. That's not the problem. I'm just not sure how I'm going to bring it back and have the days add up, but I figure I'll cross that bridge when I come to it.

At least I make Morgue's delivery in a Lexus. It gives my drug muling a little class. Maybe.

I make the drop and then drive around. Aimlessly. Yeah, driving around in my dad's car without a license is stupid, but I don't want to go home. And I have no place to go. I don't want to bother Inga, and besides, if I told her about my drug muling, I'm sure she'd lose the little respect she had for me.

I drive to Boulder and to Aurora and all the way back to Littleton, but I know all that time I'm just circling Marianne in one hell of a big radius.

She is the center of the circle. I park in front of her house, get out, walk up to the porch. Once again, I'm hoping she can save me from myself.

CHAPTER TWENTY-SIX

DOESN'T WEAR A BRA

The smell of the pines trees and the overall serenity of Marianne's neighborhood isn't calming me. The breeze knocking the dead leaves off the trees puts me further on edge. I'm thinking slippery mad thoughts a mile a minute.

It seems to me most people commit suicide like me, what I'm doing. You don't just kill yourself, you stop caring, and then you drift, and you drift into doing things that are stupid, dangerous, and plainly, as in my case, unwise. Extreme sports, drugs, crime. You either do that, or you just stop and let TV suck you down until you die in front of it. Like my grandpa did, not knowing what he was watching. Not knowing who he was. I'd walk into his room, and he'd shriek and call me the worst names imaginable. Ten letter curse words. My grandfather. Hell, with my parents and their jobs, my grandfather raised me.

Morgue's cleaver is better than the kind of death my grandfather died. And you don't need a suicide note if you die by crime. I don't care so much about my promise to Mr. Gelb, but it's my parents that trouble me. If Morgue kills me, they'll still blame themselves for not being around. I don't want that. They'll feel like Annie. Poor Dreamboat Annie and her dead brother.

I need Marianne, more than ever.

It's a little after nine. Shouldn't have been a big deal for me to knock on Marianne's door, but the house seems closed down. I go for the doorbell, and suddenly the door is open, and Marianne is out with me on the porch.

She's in her pajamas. A big man's t-shirt and blue cotton pajama bottoms with clouds on them. I can see her nipples through the shirt.

My mouth goes dry and I'm having trouble breathing. She's hot like the sun.

Marianne closes the door quietly behind her and whispers. "Jim, what are you doing? It's late. If I hadn't accidentally seen you, if you would have rung the doorbell, and my parents would've killed me. What's wrong now?"

"Nothing's wrong, Ms. Hartley," I say. MJH. My own Mary Jane. "Hey, I'm going to need your help with something."

She throws a glance back at her parents nestled in the house, and then sits on a fluffy, cushioned porch chair. She draws the t-shirt over her knees, so I can't see anything.

Pity there, but at least she's softening a little. "Sit down, Jim. What's up?"

Okay, here we go. I sit down next to her. "You know how you said that life is a gift you have to keep on giving? Well, I met this guy, and I'm not sure if I have anything to give, but I want to try." I go into it and tell her about Ray Ray and him coming to our school, and how he knew me from the greater Littleton drug-dealing community.

"So I'm going to need help," I say. "I'm not sure how far behind he is, but I want to do everything I can to make sure he gets caught up."

"How does it feel?" she asks.

I feel like the counselee again, but I shake that off. "Good. Ray Ray is a great guy." I think about him waiting for me to get into my house. And he waited for me to make sure I could get my dad's car out of the airport's long term parking.

"After band practice, let's study together," she says.

"Penumbra rules," I laugh, and make the heavy metal devil sign. "I didn't know you and 1066 knew each other."

"Who?"

I explain, Cathy Hastings, Battle of Hastings, 1066.

"How did you think I did my little donut trick?" she giggles.

I put out my hand, palm up, on her leg.

She slides her hand into my mine, and then looks at our entwined fingers. "Jim," she starts in, and I know it's not going to be something she can say with Celine Dion playing low in the background. It's not a *Jim, let's get together and love each other*. It's a, *Jim, there's a problem here.*

"What?" I ask. I have to know where I stand, even though it might feed the tiger that is currently ripping through my guts.

"Jim, I like you. But I have to go slow."

I smile. "MJH. That's how you signed your note. What's the J stand for?"

"Jennifer. It's my grandmother's name."

"We'll go real slow, MJ," I say. "I'm going to be around for a long time. I think I might have found my purpose." If the drug dealing doesn't kill me first.

She lets out a long sigh. "It's so good to hear you say that. With Brad going around betting against you."

Ask her, Jim. Ask her. Ask her about Sutter. About what he said.

I can't do it. I don't want to spoil it. With my hand in hers, I lean over and kiss her ear, very gently. I drift away into heaven on the scent of her soap, her shampoo, her own divine smell.

She shifts and kisses me, a long, sensuous, lingering kiss on my lips. Every nerve leaps and does jumping jacks inside me. I want more, I want the kiss to go deeper, but before we can get serious, she pulls away. I'm left gasping.

She's flushed and breathing hard as well. When she stands, I can see her nipples again. She catches me looking and smiles. Doesn't cover up.

"I have to get inside before my parents come looking for me," she says. "But we'll talk. We should start studying with him right off the bat. Start him off right with good study habits. Okay?"

Such a schoolgirl.

"Sure," I say, trying to get my lungs back into my chest.

She stops at the door and gives me a shy smile. "Thanks for coming over, Jim. I was drowning a little, I think."

"Head above water," I whisper, nudging my chin with the back of my hand.

She nods, gently lets the door shut, the lock clicking into place. I sit on the porch for ten minutes, trying to stop my heart from heartattacking me. I'm close to getting Marianne, but why did she pull away when the kiss was just getting good? Then why wasn't she embarrassed when she stood up? Caught me checking her out and didn't try and cover up. Is she as schoolgirl Christian as I think she is?

What Sutter said is haunting me. I have to get her full story from 1066. I have to know the truth before it kills me, now that I'm planning to live.

CHAPTER TWENTY-SEVEN

LOVE TO LIVERS

Next day at school, I'm standing in front of one of the many "Save Jim Dillenger" posters. There's this cartoonish sketch of me, heavy on the black ink, and the words, "Save Jim Dillenger" right on the front.

My school has become suicide crazy. Teachers are discussing it in every class. In English class, we take a break from *Siddhartha* to read Sylvia Plath poems. That chick lays it on a little thick. Pretty sure she was contractually obligated by her publisher to stick her head in an oven.

And then there's the assembly. The Great and Wonderful Love-To-Livers I think they are called. They actually start off the show by singing "My Favorite Things."

I sit next to 1066, trying to figure out how I can get her to talk about Marianne. Then I notice it—everyone, I mean everyone keeps turning around to see my reaction.

I stare straight at the Love-To-Livers and wonder how those actors can look at themselves in the mirror.

"Dave, don't kill yourself. Life is amazing. It's the most amazing thing there is."

Poor, depressed Dave. "What's so great about it?"

Cue poorly played piano. *Raindrops on daises and whiskers on puppies.* Or something like that. *Kill me now.*

Finally, the assembly ends with a bang, and I latch onto 1066. "Ten, uh, what do you do for lunch?"

Todd and his crew are shouting about wanting to see another assembly called "The Great and Wonderful We-Hate-Our-Livers". Todd starts singing his version of "My Favorite Things."

Retards on buses and dope fiends on acid.

For a minute, I miss my friends. Until Todd looks at me again, and does his whole finger to the temple thing. I don't get it. Is it for me to shoot myself, or for him to shoot himself?

1066 watches the bridge crew walk away down the hall. Then she answers my question. "Sometimes at lunch I eat with Marianne, but lately I've been going to the music room to play piano. Want to come with me?"

I nod. Sure, hang out with the fat girl for a while.

On the way over, 1066 is eating her sandwich, and I walk with her. I have to ask. "So, Ten, what about Marianne? We had a moment last night. I gotta know. Does she have a boyfriend?"

"Not anymore."

Could it be? Sutter and Marianne? Again, didn't compute. But I ask anyway. "Was it Brad Sutter? Was she going out with Brad Sutter?"

Ten shrugs. "I can't say."

"You said she kinda had a boyfriend. Was she kinda seeing Sutter? Was it supposed to be a secret because Sutter didn't want it to get out?" I'm hoping against hope that Ten will say Marianne has been seeing Jesus, but it didn't work out.

Ten doesn't. She confirms it. "I guess it's okay now, but you can't tell anyone about Marianne and Brad, okay?"

"Yeah."

We get to the band room, and go in. Nobody home. "It's okay. Mrs. Shapiro knows about me coming in." Ten says it like I need permission.

She sits down at the piano. "Marianne showed me some things, and I've just been practicing them. I'm not good, so don't make fun of me."

"Not me, no way, uh huh," I say.

She starts playing something, slow. I think it's Elton John or Billy Joel or Bruce Hornsby. Aren't they all the same person? Ten puts them all to shame.

"What do you think?" she asks, stopping.

I have to smile. "If that's not good, you must rock on your bass."

"Totally rock," she says with a big, confident smile, and for a minute, I see who she'll become. She's not there yet, but I can see it. She'll be gorgeous when she gets there.

"Do you sing too?" I ask.

She plays again, and then she stops. "Sometimes. They all want me to sing more, but I could never do it in front of people. Doug sings. He's pretty good."

My Doug?

Before I can register it might be the same guy, 1066 keeps talking. "One of my heroes is Geddy Lee from Rush. He sings, plays bass, and does keyboards. He's amazing. Maybe someday."

Geddy what from who? I ignore that, and go back to my favorite topic. "Tell me about Marianne."

Ten looks at the piano for a long time, and then answers. "Marianne's parents are super- strict, and she doesn't like people talking about her at school, and so she keeps things secret. Like with Brad."

"Sutter said she would break my heart," I say.

Ten shrugs. Her fingers tumble across the keys. "Marianne is nice, and I don't want to talk bad about her, but…sometimes…"

Mrs. Shapiro comes in, crosses the room to her desk, and then pauses to look at us. "Jim Dillenger in my classroom. I should ask for your autograph or something."

"I'm not serious," I say. I say that all the time. Methinks I protest too much.

She pauses, and then comes over. She shows me her wrist. "I wasn't serious either," she says.

I see the faded scars on her wrist. Mrs. Shapiro is a trip. Coolest teacher around.

"Funny how not serious can still leave scars and land you in the hospital." She pulls her sleeve back down.

Dang. I'm speechless for a minute, but I return to my favorite question. "What keeps you going, Mrs. Shapiro?"

She smiles. "Triathlons. Do not underestimate the wonderful world of sports-induced endorphins. When all else fails, move your large muscle groups."

"Better living through exercise," I quip.

She doesn't quip back. Instead, she gets serious. "You'll have to choose at some point, Jim, whether you want to live or die. I wish you luck with that."

She takes off.

"Dang," I say.

Ten just plays the piano, and I listen, watching her face, thinking about Marianne, thinking about Morgue. Thinking.

I have to go pick up my money from K-Zee, Morgue's very yellow-clothed assistant. I'm not looking forward to it.

CHAPTER TWENTY-EIGHT

JUST KEEPING IT REAL

In my dad's car, I drive to Morgue' restaurant, park, and as I'm walking up, I finally figure out how to look at the sign so I can see what the restaurant is called. It's called Sinastra. Left in Latin. Where we get sinister.

I pause for a minute, wondering what in the hell I'm doing, but then I go inside.

The restaurant is empty. The black guy behind the bar looks at me, and then jerks his head toward the hallway without saying a word.

Down the hall, in the manager's office, there's K-Zee in yellow. He hands me an envelope. "Nice job, cracker. You didn't jack it up. We'll call you when we need you again." He goes back to standing over the desk, moving papers.

I see the window behind him. This is the right spot. This is where the Halloween drop will be. I remember the scars on Mrs. Shapiro's wrist. I remember Marianne's hair and the curve of her ear and her smell. Our kiss. I think about what Ray Ray said. What Inga said. And then I say to K-Zee, "What if I don't want another job?"

He stops shuffling papers and looks at me. It's a rattlesnake stare. "Don't mess with us, cracker. This ain't no game. This ain't no job you can quit. You in or out, right now. You tell me. Right now. In or out?"

"In," I say. "I just wanted to check my options."

"Check your options on your own time, cracker. Now get out of here. We'll call you."

I leave.

In the envelope is a thousand dollars all for me. For a simple little drive. If they can give me that much money for just a little drop, how much money will be there on Halloween night? Millions.

I give the attendant at the airport's long-term parking a hundred dollars from the drug money to adjust the computer so my dad will pay his normal fee. Dang, I grease his palm like I'm used to bribing people.

I take the bus home and I turn off my head. Just flick the switch. I'm done thinking. I have a ton of money. Hell, another drop I can buy some used piece-of-rust car to do my drug dealing.

"It's not drug dealing," I say to myself. I need to say it out loud. I need to hear myself say it. "Not drug dealing at all. It's some kind of wussy suicide, Jim. That's all it is."

Mrs. Shapiro said I needed to decide whether I wanted to live or die. Well, K-Zee made me decide, and I still chose death.

What would the Love-To-Livers say about that?

I can ask Ray Ray. He's shooting baskets in front of my house. His white Escalade is nowhere to be seen.

CHAPTER TWENTY-NINE

RACE RELATIONS AND TRAGEDIES IN AMERICA

"I'm ready for school, King," Ray Ray says to me as I walk up. He bounces the ball to me.

"Uh, Ray, don't know if you can just start…"

He looks at me, then at the ball. "You gonna shoot?"

I completely miss the basket, and the ball winds up dribbling off the roof.

Ray holds up his hands, and I see two things I had missed before. His eye is bruised, and his left hand is bandaged up. I can see a little dried blood on the ace bandage covering his pinky.

"What happened to you?" I ask.

"You can't just walk away from Morgue," Ray Ray says. "But I got off easy. Maybe you leave now, you'll get off easy too."

I throw him the ball, and he catches it with his right hand and makes a nice jump shot.

"I'm always going to feel bad about getting you into it," Ray Ray says. "Quit now, man. Give it up before it's too late."

"Ray, man, I chose all of this," I say. And I keep choosing it, I add in my head.

"Still, I should've told you to stay away. Shame on me." He stops shooting baskets, and we sit in the grass.

The autumn sun is going down, and the sky is filled with a weak light that hides as much as it reveals. The grass is drying out, getting ready for winter.

I let Ray talk. I don't have much to say anyway.

"You think I'm some hood rat, huh? Some "g" on the street in a gang, dealing and doing drive-bys. It's not like that. I'm not like that."

I have to point out the socio-economic realities. "Ray, you know you're going to get that at school, right? Not a lot of racial diversity in this neck of the woods."

He shrugs and then tells me his life story. "My mom and my dad were teachers. Hell, they weren't just teachers, they were professors. My dad grew up rough in Oakland, but my mom came from here, from a good family. They met in school, taught at colleges in California, had a family. My brother took after my dad, always in trouble, just not satisfied with anything. When my parents died, I came out here to live with him. At first, he was like, go to school, study hard, don't follow in my footsteps. But I didn't have exactly any discipline around to make sure I did my homework or even got out of bed in the morning. And one thing led to another, and here I am."

He raises his bandaged hand. "I got out easy. Most of me made it out. My brother didn't. He's dead."

"Ray, it's going to take a while to get you into school," I say. "And where's your Escalade?"

"Re-possessed," he says with a smile. "I don't want to do no foster home, King. I'm kinda counting on you for everything."

The enormity of the whole situation settles into my guts, and it makes me want to puke. He's talking about moving in. I'm going to become his illegal guardian.

I have to laugh. "Man, this teacher I had, he used to talk about white guilt, and how white people want to help the black man, but it's a bad setup. Like charity or whatever. He used to call it the misguided liberal agenda. I guess this is a white liberal's dream."

He laughs. "Yeah, if you would've told me a week ago I'd be needing a place to live in Littleton, I'd have put my foot in your ass."

"This kind of thing doesn't happen." I echo his own words back to him. No, it doesn't. Not to me. Not to anyone. How did I get here? What happened to my life?

Ray Ray laughs. "That's what I said. But here we are. You still suicidal?"

"You still want to go to school?" I ask.

"I'm betting everything on it," he says as the last line of sunlight disappears behind the mountains.

We have a guest room in the basement, so Ray can stay there. It's really private, and we have a back door he can use. My grandpa used to live there before he went to the home.

Yeah, eventually I'll have to tell my dad the whole story about Ray. With my mom setting herself up in Cleveland, my dad is trying to spend more time at home, but he's still mostly gone. Which means Ray can stay in our basement untouched for a long time.

That first night, I'm sitting at my desk trying to do homework in my prison cell of a bedroom. Ray Ray is in the basement, worlds away, with the washer going. I'm doing laundry because Goodwill won't be open before school in the morning. Laundry, another reason why life is too hard, but I need to just accept the fact I have to replace my stuff and get over it.

My parents call, concerned about me because friends of theirs heard about the "Save Jim Dillenger" posters at school. I have a sneaky suspicion Mrs. Farmer is responsible for the posters, but I can't let myself care. When my parents ask me if I'm okay, this time I can be truthful. Me? Suicidal? I have everything to live for. Well, maybe not everything, but I have Ray now. I don't tell them about him. Not yet.

Shaky after easing my parents out of flying home immediately, I call Marianne. I give her the latest on Ray, and she's blown away, but committed to help.

Then we talk about everything and nothing for three, wonderful, beautiful hours.

Midnight, I hang up the phone.

Okay, it's easy. K-Zee calls, and I say no.

Let's practice.

K-Zee says to me, "Hey, cracker, come and deal drugs and make money and become some vassal for a psychotic, gangland baron."

"No."

Easy. Sure.

I'm getting ready for bed when I hear the window shatter downstairs. For being a guy on the edge, I freeze up and pray it's not Morgue coming for me and Ray Ray.

In the movies, you see the hero always dashing around when the proverbial manure hits the air conditioning. In real life it doesn't work like that. Not for me. There's just a lot of standing around, wondering what to do.

There I am, standing by my bed, trying to convince myself I hadn't heard anything although I know I did—glass shattering and car tires screaming away.

I'm wondering if there are intruders in my house, and how fast I can call the cops, when I hear Ray call up to me. "Yo, King, you awake?"

I go out into the hall and look over the banister down to Ray who is standing in the dining room. In his good hand he has a huge semi-automatic pistol. In his bandaged hand is a note. A brick and several rubber bands are on the dining room table.

"Not me," he says. "Can't blame this on the brother man, but on the other man. It's for you, King." He has the wrinkled piece of paper in his hand.

I come down and he hands me the note.

It says in bad, jock handwriting:

ISN'T IT ABOUT TIME YOU KILLED YOURSELF?

"Yeah," I say. "It's for me. My not-so-secret admirer."

CHAPTER THIRTY

'CAUSE RAY RAY IS HERE TO STAY

Long story short, Ray gets into school. My dad stays gone through the weekend, and on Monday, I take Ray to school with me. Mr. Gelb and Mrs. Farmer are true to their word, and even though all the paperwork hasn't gone through, when he and I show up, the administration doesn't send him away. Ray ends up in a lot of classes with Todd and the old crew. Which is good because they all know each other. And it's bad because they all know each other.

Ray Ray and I go over things as we walk home from school that first day. He says he's not even tempted. "I didn't come out here to get stoned with white versions of black friends I still have. Now that would be messed up."

"How's Todd doing?" I ask.

Ray shrugs. "That fool's crazy. He says you don't have the balls to kill yourself, but he does."

Ah, Todd. Always so competitive.

"You should probably get rid of your gun," I say.

"Yeah, but it's hard. Gift from my brother. And I don't know, you get used to it. Like a security blanket."

I laugh at that. "A dangerous security blanket. And you know me, I'm not trusted around dangerous objects."

Ray nods. "Maybe we'll need it to scare off Sutter. Get him to give up his drive-bys."

I'm not worried about Sutter.

I'm worried about K-Zee calling.

Ray brings me back to reality. "So, do you study right away, or what? How does this work?"

It's a good question. "Well, Ray, here's the thing. Usually, I would go get loaded with Todd under the bridge, and then go home, watch TV, and when I'm coming out of it, I would study until midnight. Up at seven to brush my teeth and go to school. That was my routine."

"Good thing you didn't do crack, King. You got that addict way about you."

I slap Ray on the back. "Amen to that, R2. Amen to that."

We study and do homework at my kitchen table. I can't help but notice that Ray is moving his lips while he reads. But he's serious. God help me, he's serious about school.

At one point, he stops and just starts laughing. He can't stop himself, and he's just laughing and laughing.

"What?" I keep asking.

He's wiping tears away from his eyes. "I was scared. I was scared of doing homework. Ha, this ain't nothing, King. This ain't nothing. So this is school. After all the shit I've been through, this ain't nothing at all."

"No, man, it ain't nothing, R2."

Later on, I call Marianne and we come up with a plan. Ray and I will go and watch her band practice, and then we'll all go study. A new routine for me and Ray.

I settle in for a three-hour call, and Marianne pulls the plug.

"I gotta go," she says. I think I can hear someone talking in the background. Doubts rise, but I wipe them aside. I will have Marianne. Of course I will. I'm the bad boy she can save, and Ray is all thanks to her in a roundabout way. She'll see what I'm doing for Ray and be completely impressed and I'll get another kiss, this time of the French variety.

I hang up, and again practice saying no when K-Zee calls. With Ray to take care of, and Marianne to get, I have too much to live for to just throw it away.

I'm about to go to bed when I remember about Inga, her surgery, her mail. I go down the stairs and outside, to grab my mail and hers. Her mailbox is empty, no notes for me, nothing. She's too cool for me to just drop her. I vow to bring Ray over, or write her a note, to thank her I guess.

I have a purpose now. New friends. I'm backing away from the edge, and I'm glad. Bottom line, if you stand too close to the edge for too long, only a matter of time before you slip off.

CHAPTER THIRTY-ONE

IS DOING FINE ON CLOUD NINE

After school, Ray Ray and I walk over to Marianne's church. Our Lady of Perpetual Sorrow, or whatever. It's a Roman Catholic church, though it looks more like the compound for a cult rather than your typical cathedral. Lots of square buildings cast about around a larger square with a cross at the very top. It's like the evil anti-Notre Dame. Inside, we accidentally stumble into the sanctuary where Jesus is suffering dutifully on his cross, right where he is supposed to be.

Ray stops to glance at the crucifix and the stained glass windows. Empty pews wait patiently in the silence. For what, I have no idea.

"You believe in God, King?" Ray asks.

"Depends on what kind of God you have in mind, Ray," I answer, which isn't much of an answer.

"I do, man," Ray says. "Hard to believe all of this doesn't mean nothing."

"Yeah," I say, completely noncommittal.

"So if you believe in God, how do you think He feels about you and all of this suicide?" Ray asks.

"I think it's more important about how I feel towards Him," I answer with some force. "He sets up this nightmare world and then takes off. What has He done for me lately?"

"You something, King," Ray says, laughing.

We keep walking until we hear music, from below us. 1066's band practices in the church basement. When they aren't working on songs for the Youth Mass, they play real music. Ray and I stop at the doorway. I see Doug sitting there with his guitar, some short-haired muscular guy is at the drums, and there's Marianne playing a keyboard. They are all watching 1066.

She's singing. She has her bass slung over her shoulder, she's at the microphone, and I can't believe it, but my Ten is singing, and she's not just singing shyly or all uncomfortable, which is what I would expect. No, dude, she's giving it her all. Like she's the next American Idol. Marianne is playing along, but Ten doesn't need it.

Her eyes are closed, and I see that confidence she hides. That beauty. Who knew she could sing like that?

Under his breath, Ray whispers, "She's good."

It's a song about crying to heaven, and I feel a shiver on the back of my neck.

She finishes, and there's this silence in the room.

Then Ten comes right back. The Ten I know and love, so to speak. "What?" she asks.

Doug is shaking his head. "You have got to sing that for the Youth Mass this Sunday. It's amazing. You're amazing."

Ten turns ten shades of purple. "I couldn't. Not in front of other people."

"You did it in front of them." Marianne waves at Ray and me in the doorway.

A shocked Ten turns to look at us. "No, I can't. I can't." She gets all flustered, and starts packing up her bass.

"No, just one more song," I say.

"If it isn't the Suicide King," Doug says. "Good to see you above ground."

"Duh, duh, Doug," I stutter violently. "Good to see you. Tortured any Jews lately?"

There's this long, uncomfortable pause, like they are all trying to register what I said, and why I said it.

Even though she's still packing up her things, Ten gets it and takes away the awkward silence. "He's talking about the Inquisition, when the Church—"

"I know," Doug says a little cprinturtly. "That's your problem, Jim. You can cast stones. You can make fun of other people's faith, but what do you believe in besides death?"

I come into the room. "Okay, I'll preach it. Can I get a witness? I believe in Marianne Hartley," I say, and I kind of trip on that, but I keep going. "I believe that good ol' Cathy Hastings can sing like an angel. I believe in my new friend Ray Ray who is college bound, by God. I believe in radio, television, and films. I believe that life is far more weird without drugs than with them. I believe the first beer of the night is the best beer, but not even an ocean of booze can slake my great thirst. I believe that maybe when you're drowning, trying to help other people stay above water, well, it just might save us all."

If I've gotten anything out of this suicide trip, it's the ability to say what I'm really thinking without squeaking like a mouse.

The others are kind of taken by my speech, but of course Doug is unimpressed. "And God doesn't take any credit for any of that?"

"Fuck God." It's the next logical thing to say. I've said both of those words a lot in my life. Seemed logical to put them together.

"Jim, you're in a church," Marianne gasps.

I'm oddly serene. "Yeah, and if there is a God, you'd think He'd strike me dead for being such a rude guest in His house, but hey,

I'm thinking about coming to church just to see you play. You guys are great."

Tried to change the subject, but, well, no. It's not going down that way.

Doug always has something to say. "I think you're going to find God, Jim. Anyone who thinks about this stuff as much as you will surely find the truth."

"Yeah," I exaggerate the word. "Anyway…"

Ray, all class, knows just what to do. "We only got to hear one song. How about another one?"

"Cathy, can you stop packing for just a minute?" Marianne asks Ten. The color is still high on Ten's face. "You were great. Why are you so embarrassed?"

"How about we do 'YYZ'?" Doug suggests.

"That's bribery." Ten sighs and picks up her bass. "Okay. Okay. But we don't have to do a Rush song. We can play a request. What would you guys like to hear?"

When asked, I always say 'Free Bird,' though I'm not sure why.

Ray speaks up. "What kind of old school do you know? Like old R&B?"

Leave it to Ten. "I've been trying to get them to play some Temptations. They said no to Parliament."

Ray laughs and shakes his head.

Ten blushes further. "I'm a bassist. I mean, that old 70s funk relied a lot on bass."

"Yeah, yeah, I know," Ray says, "It's just funny that you guys know that stuff. I wouldn't have expected it."

"Let's try 'Cloud Nine'," Doug says.

They start, and it's not my style, not enough gnashing guitars and angst, but it's okay. Ten is amazing on her bass. Doug sings, and even he's good. Not bad, not bad at all. Ten would have sung it much better though.

Maybe I'll start playing guitar, and oust Doug. Suddenly life is full of possibilities.

Once the song is over, Rays claps while he laughs. "You guys were great," he says to them. Under his breath, he whispers to me, "That was the whitest version of that song ever done."

They pack up while Marianne leaves to go get her car, to load up her gear. Ray goes with her. Not sure how that happened, but I'm cool with it. They can get to know each other. Once Marianne sees how epic Ray is, she'll like me even more for helping him out.

Out of nowhere, 1066 grabs my arm. "I want to show you something."

I let her pull me along. Why not? I liked *The Da Vinci Code*. I'm hoping for juicy Catholic heresies. Instead, 1066 shows me a courtyard in the middle of the church. A fountain gurgles, hidden by plants and leafy trees. Benches are scattered around. In the middle of the garden is a statue of Jesus, eyes up at the sky. He doesn't look hip or happy. He looks troubled.

I'm oddly moved. Inga's rebel theology comes back. We're all Jesus.

"They modeled this place after a garden in the Gospel, where Jesus doubted God, right before he was arrested."

Somehow I know the name of the garden. "Gethsemane," I whisper. Seems like the only proper thing to do, whisper. Maybe I shouldn't have cursed in the church, but nothing about the church felt sacred except for this little courtyard garden.

"Do you feel it?" 1066 asks in a hush.

I want to say something sarcastic. I want to shrug off this superstitious nonsense, but I can't help myself. She's right. I do feel something. I shiver a little. And feel really, really insignificant.

"Yeah, Ten, I feel it. I wish I could believe like you and Marianne, but I just can't."

"You don't have to believe anything. Maybe what we believe isn't important. Maybe it's more about what we feel. Like this place. There's really nothing special about it, but then, there is. I come here to pray because of how it feels."

I can argue against emotional Christianity all day long. Less emotions plus more logic equals less murdering. A little logic would've done the Crusaders some good. I don't attack 1066, though. What's the point of me giving anyone a history lesson? Nothing. We stand in silence for a minute, and then we walk out to the parking lot where Ray is loading up Marianne's car.

Doug and the other band members are gone, so it's just Ray, me, Marianne and 1066. We all pile in. I somehow wind up in the back seat with Ten. Ray is in the front with Marianne, and they're talking about Marianne's music, and her religion, and they're getting along great. I was a little worried, but Marianne keeps laughing. I can see she likes Ray.

Good. That's good. Ten will always just be along for the ride, and so our foursome study group should work out. Cool.

Ten looks at me underneath the pile of backpacks and musical instruments teetering on our laps and scraping the ceiling. Her eyes are blue. Blue like sky-blue heaven. I had never noticed before.

"Tell me the truth. Was I any good?" she asks. Back to being the shy, fat girl.

"Ten, you were awesome," I say, though I know she would never believe it. "Even Gary Lee would have been impressed."

Ten giggles. "Geddy Lee."

"Yeah, him too."

We go back to my house and crowd around the kitchen table, unloading books and paper and pens. At one point, I get up to go to the bathroom, and when I come back, I see all of my little chicks studying at my table, and I feel proud that I could get them all together. That I could create such a cool situation.

I think about what Doug said, about not giving God any credit. If Marianne hadn't given me the whole idea of giving away my life, none of this would've happened.

I could never have planned any of it.

Maybe there is a God.

Maybe life can be good.

At that moment, I don't want to kill myself. The idea of death seems as far away as Greenland.

Leave it to Greenland to come and punch me in the face.

CHAPTER THIRTY-TWO

PUNCHES AND NO HELP

For two weeks I'm flittering about on cloud nine. One afternoon I introduce Ray to Inga during a postal run. We're holding her mail and she is leaning on her cane in the doorway while smiling lovey-dovey at my new friend. "Well, Ray, now you look like a sensible young man. Why are you hanging out with the neighborhood's Suicide King?"

Ray shrugs. "I like to help white kids when I can."

Her smile curls up at the corners as she invites us in and uses her cane to get to the dining room table where she plops down. Ray wanders around, lost in the Louvre pretending to be Inga's living room.

I sit down at the table with her. "Inga, come on, how can you possibly know about my nickname? And I'm not serious. If I were, I would've kept it way more secret."

I'm thinking she's telepathic, but instead, she heard about me from the granddaughter of a friend of hers. "But, James, something has changed. Where has your *Weltschmertz* gone? What has changed?"

I can't help but glance over at Ray, who is cradling a dusty atlas.

She touches my arm. "And a girl, I would suppose. You look a little dizzy."

"A ton of stuff has happened. I can't quite get my head wrapped around it all. Yeah, things are good."

"I am so glad, James, so very glad. This life can be very challenging, my friend, and at times, it can play very unfair."

"What about you?" I ask. "Do you have a surgery date?"

"Next month. Don't worry, I have my friends who'll come and get my mail and to take care of me. I know you are very busy living your teenage life. So many important things to be done when you are young." She pats my arm like it's so hard being me. Why did she love to tease me? She calls to Ray, "Do you have dreams of traveling, young man? You look smitten with that atlas."

"It's just so old. I'm trying to figure out where Prussia is. But yeah, I would like to travel someday. Like around the world. Thailand, Africa, Italy, Brazil. That'd be cool."

"Hot, mostly, the places you mentioned. Has James told you about my very exciting life?"

"A little," Ray says. "So you were like a doctor?"

"Yes, almost like a doctor, a surgeon, but close enough." She smiles at him.

"No, I didn't mean like a doctor," Ray says, getting a little flustered. Where did Mr. Cool Eyes go?

Inga laughs. "You boys, so silly, so very silly."

We chat more, and Inga flirts with Ray more than me. Which makes me oddly jealous.

"So glad your *Weltschmertz* seems to be in remission," Inga says to me as we leave her house. "I have prayed for you every day, James, and my heart feels very full to see you happy."

I wave goodbye as I take Ray away.

"Nice meeting you!" Ray calls over his shoulder. Then to me, "I have never met anyone like that in my life. Dang. She makes me want to try every new thing I can."

I know how he feels.

My life has become one huge new thing. Ray, our study group, and a whole new, clean routine. School, band practice, studying, dinner, sleep, repeat. I keep insisting that Ten sing every afternoon, which she does after a lot of coercing. She even does "Cloud Nine" with the band, and it's better, blacker.

They always go back to The Offspring and Green Day covers. Ray Ray just shakes his head. White kids.

I gotta give it to Doug, though. He can hammer his ax like a madman and still sing pretty. Impressive. And he starts being nicer to me. Not so confrontational.

Yeah, it's all cherry and getting redder. I even use my drug money to buy more clothes, off the rack at Macy's. All my old clothes are gone from Goodwill, which is a testament to my fashion sense.

In uncontaminated outfits, with new friends, with Marianne giving me smiles that would melt cheese, it's all good until the Wednesday before Halloween. My mom is due back the first of November, and my dad changed his schedule so they'd both be home at the same time. A happy, disintegrating family.

While my dad is around, we set Ray Ray up at a local motel, using money from my first and so far only experience of drug muling. He doesn't trust himself to be back with his old friends in Denver. I don't blame him a bit.

K-Zee hasn't called yet, but I know it's coming. I get myself ready to say I'm done, so sorry, gonna have to find another little mule.

I'm practicing my quitting speech on that Wednesday, when Sutter finds me after school. I'm alone, walking to meet Ray. Sutter is worried about his five hundred bucks and the fact that the "Save Jim Dillenger" posters seem to be working.

Out behind the portable classrooms, Sutter and I do our old dance step.

Push, two, three, four.

Wall, two, three, four.

Fist, two, three, four.

"You gotta be dying soon, man." Sutter spits when he talks. He's the spitter, and I'm the spittee.

"Gross," I say.

He punches me in the gut.

He stands over me, and this time it's just me and his friends. Jocks travel in packs, don't you know, like wolves, with the alpha male strutting his stuff.

"So what's your deal, Dillenger? You living for Marianne? If I didn't have a deadline, I'd just let her kill you. Which she will."

One of his buddies says something about Sutter keeping a secret, and Sutter just shrugs it off.

He picks me up and it's back against the wall. "You don't kill yourself, Dillenger, tomorrow I'm going to make you pray for death. Me and my homies."

"How do you spell that?" Ray asks.

He's leaning up against the portable unit, looking at us.

I'm nearly dripping with gratitude. Old Ray is going to bodyguard up and save the day.

Sutter turns away from me. "Leave us alone," he says. "This is private."

"Hey, this is the black guy who Dillenger got into our school," one of the jocks says.

"But can it even read?" Sutter spits.

I smile. Now he's going to get it. I'm hoping Ray has his gun.

"I asked you to spell 'homie' and you can't answer me," Ray says. "Maybe you can't read."

Sutter throws me into the arms of his compadres, and I hang there, waiting for Ray to throw his first punch. Or draw his gun. Either way, we're going to go ghetto on their asses.

Sutter is in Ray's face.

Ray's eyes are mad-dog blank.

It's on like Donkey Kong.

"Are we going to do this?" Sutter asks.

Ray shakes his head. "Nope. I ain't doing nothin'. I can't get kicked out of school. I can just watch, and then just tell 'em what I saw."

"What about running to get help?" Sutter asks, breathing hard. I can almost smell the adrenaline oozing out of his pores.

Ray smirks. "And you're gonna let me run off? I don't think so. And what you're gonna do to Jim ain't gonna take that long."

Sutter nods. "They're training hoodrats smart nowadays," he says, and walks back to me.

He throws a look at Ray. "So you aren't going to stop me even if I do this." He then hits me hard in the stomach.

I can't breathe, and I'm sucking wind like a fish on the sand. Then I panic. I struggle against their arms with every fear-driven muscle I have, but they hold on to me, too strong for me to get away.

Ray still has nothing on his face. Then he smiles. Then he laughs. "Sutter, you ever watch those high school movies and think to yourself, 'I'm just like all them bullies.' I gotta say, you do 'em right. But don't you feel dumb? You do know those are the bad guys, right?"

Sutter gives him a grimace and hits me right in the face. My face throbs with pain. My blood splatters across my cheeks.

"And why are you doing this again, Sutter?" Ray asks.

I'm in pain and I'm afraid, but I still get pissed at my buddy. He's letting me get beat up, not doing a damn thing to help me.

Sutter shakes his head. "I got five hundred dollars riding on Dillenger killing himself before Halloween. I'm just giving him some incentive."

Ray grins. "And you're going to help him along. Like assisted suicide."

Sutter likes that. "Yeah, I'm his own personal Dr. Kevorkian." Sutter flexes, and I'm praying, not the face, not the face, not the face.

Yeah, once again in the face. I'm an earthquake of pain with my nose as the epicenter.

Ray keeps asking his questions, like he's a prosecuting attorney, clarifying the crime while it's being committed. "And you're going to keep messin' with Jim until he gives up and kills himself?"

Sutter snickers. "Yeah. Another couple of beatings, and he'll find a way. He's so smart, after all."

I don't feel smart at that point.

"Hey, a custodian's coming over," one of the jocks says, and the whole posse flees, leaving me on the ground.

In my own blood.

Ray tries to help me up. I push his hands away. "I can't believe you just stood there."

"Come on, Jim, there were five of them. All that would've happened is that we both would be bleeding. And if we had been caught, I would've been expelled. You know that's true. Gelb is looking for any excuse to get rid of me."

It all makes sense, but it feels too good to just lie on my back, swallow blood, and hate him for a minute. He could have saved the day. He could have paid me back for all that I had done for him.

I keep thinking what my mom always says, *No good deed ever goes unpunished.*

Then Ray gives me some hope. "I'll take care of Sutter. Don't worry. It'll be a little surprise for you. Give you an incentive to keep on living."

My hate diminishes a little. I'm thinking drive-by as I pull myself up. Good, maybe instead of suicide, I can get into homicide. Hopefully less of my blood will be spilled.

"I can't go home like this," I say.

Ray has a black t-shirt under his jacket. He peels both off, and then hands me the t-shirt. "Here, man. I'm sorry I couldn't help. It felt messed up, watching him do that to you."

I press the t-shirt against my nose to stop the blood.

"We can clean you up at Marianne's house," Ray says. "Her parents aren't going to be home until late, and I knew we couldn't use your pad, so we're going to study over at her house."

Marianne and Ray had talked at school. Okay, that's cool, but still, it didn't help me in my current bloody state.

"Did you even have your gun?" I ask.

Ray shakes his head. "No, man, I got to thinking about it. They got that zero tolerance thing, and if I get caught with it, I'd be gone. So I hid it in my room at your house."

He wouldn't have had to hide it well. I know my dad wouldn't be doing anything with the guest room.

"So you're serious about staying in school?" I ask Ray, looking for a little sunshine in the day.

"This is my one shot," Ray says. "I'm gonna hold on tight to it."

For a minute, I feel like Jesus. Maybe Inga is right. Jesus suffered and died for mankind, and I took a beating for my friend Ray. He's really trying, and I wanted him to throw it all away just so I wouldn't get hit again.

Sutter isn't worth it. Sutter isn't worth anything.

But in the end, I had a worse pounding coming to me.

CHAPTER THIRTY-THREE

PIECES OF SILVER

We hit Marianne's house, and it's ice packs and washcloths and Brad Sutter this and oh-my-God that. Ray keeps his jacket on, unzipped, showing off his abs. Marianne and 1066 keep glancing at him. I consider taking off my own shirt, but really, I couldn't compete.

"I just have to lay low until Halloween," I say. "That's when the betting pool ends. It's not a big deal."

"I'll stop him," Marianne says with this ferocity I've not seen before. "It's about me more than anything."

Ray looks at her. I watch him stare at her. Could it be?

Marianne whisks brown hair behind her ear. "Why else would he be doing this?"

1066 just lowers her head and starts working on her homework.

"You hooked up with that asshole?" Ray asks, completely shocked.

I want to see how she will answer. I move the washcloth a little to look at her face. She's crimson.

"It was stupid," she said. "I know, I know. It just happened, and it got worse, and I didn't know how to get out of it."

Sure. Marianne felt like she was drowning, and so she breaks up with Sutter to hook up with me. That's why Sutter came after me, and that's why he said the things he had said.

Sure.

Except 1066 has her head lowered and is studying like a fiend. Methinks she studies too much.

What really happened?

"Don't worry," Ray says with a big smile on his face. "I got it all taken care of. That guy won't be bothering the King no more."

Then 1066 can't help it. "Anymore," she whispers.

"Anymore," Ray says, correcting himself. "Got that double-negative beat, baby. I ain't gonna say it no more. Not no more."

"Right," Marianne says with a big smile on her face.

All this smiling. Ray does know that Marianne and I are a thing? Maybe a fetal thing, the prototype of a thing, but we have something. Ray knows that, right?

Then my phone rings. It's my dad calling. His voice is flat. Hard. "Jim, I found blood on the sheets in the guest room. No BS this time. Tell me what happened."

Damn, Ray had cleared out his stuff and dumped the trash, but I hadn't thought of changing the sheets. The blood would be from Ray's hand, though I still hadn't seen underneath the bandage. What's my dad doing in the guest room anyway? Can't I get a break on anything?

I walk out of Marianne's kitchen into their official dining room and then into the unused living room by the front door. There are pictures of Jesus everywhere. I feel His eyes following me waiting for me to cuss again so he can strike me dead. Everything un-Jesus is lacy, kitty cute.

"What were you doing in the guest room?" I ask my dad, trying to think up something.

"When your mother gets home, I'll be sleeping there. I figured I might do some laundry, and then I found the sheets. And what happened to your room? Where are all your posters? All your books? Did you buy all new clothes? Where did you get the money for that? When you get home, I want the truth. Everything."

He pauses.

"Was it your blood, Jim? Were you hurting yourself?"

Man, it hurts, him asking me those questions. I have a flashback of Dreamboat Annie, about her brother. Suicide is the ultimate selfish act. That's clear. But my Suicide King popularity, this broadcasting of suicide, is just as selfish. I can hear from my dad's voice that it tears him up to ask those questions. Suicides don't just kill themselves—they murder the people who love them as well.

"No," I say to my dad. "No, dad, it wasn't my blood. We'll talk. As for my room, when Todd and I broke up, I needed a new start and so I got rid of everything. It's no big deal. You'll see."

I hang up, feeling guilty about the pain I'm causing my dad, but proud of the lie about my room. Even if I'm getting better at lying, I know at some point, I'm going to have to come clean with my dad about Ray.

I walk back into the kitchen, and there's 1066 doing homework. She looks up, and I see something there, some subtle thing on her face.

"Where's Ray and Marianne?" I ask.

Her eyes shift upstairs, for a second, an instant. Before she shrugs again.

I feel the truth, solid, in my stomach. Right in the very center of my colon.

My soul knows, but my eyes need convincing.

I turn to walk away, but 1066 stops me by finally talking. "Look, Jim, Marianne isn't bad. She's just..." She can't finish the thought. So she says what is completely logical. "You two were never really together, right?"

"We kissed," I say, but it's like I'm spitting into the wind. The kiss meant a lot to me, but to Marianne?

"What happened with Sutter?" I ask.

1066 grips her pencil tighter. She lowers her head. "If I tell you, will you come back and study?"

"Sure." I love that word. It's a one-syllable way to lie.

"Sutter caught Marianne with his best friend at a party. She was trying to get out of her thing with Sutter, and well, she really liked Logan, but then she moved on to Tyler."

My brain tries to catalogue all the names, while my heart implodes. I'm surprised I'm still standing. If Marianne has found a sluttier way of avoiding drowning, well, I have to see it for myself.

"Sorry, Ten, totally lied to you." I walk away. She doesn't come after me.

Okay, Marianne might be a total whore-bag, but what about Ray? He wouldn't sell me out for thirty pieces of silver, would he? Did he go all ghetto-Judas on me?

I creep like a cat up the stairs, hoping I'm wrong. Hoping and praying I'm as wrong as I can be.

Praying to Marianne's God.

There's only one closed door. I walk down the hall, my stomach jumping with every step. My hand is shaking when I reach for the door. I quietly, oh–so-quietly open it.

The hinges are oiled silence. The door swings open and there's my buddy Ray, on Marianne's pink bedspread, with her underneath him. Grinding.

I close the door silently.

Inside, I take my care button and rip it out by the wires. I back away, tiptoe down the steps, and charge out the front door, leaving 1066 to study her little heart out in the kitchen. I don't take my backpack with me. I don't need it anymore. I'm done with school. Done with everything.

On the front porch, where Marianne and I had our one and only kiss, my phone rings.

I know who it is.

It can only be one person. In yellow. K-Zee is on the other end. I can almost hear the neon of his outfit in his voice. "Hey, cracker, you ready for another job?"

"I was born ready," I say.

CHAPTER THIRTY-FOUR

SUICIDE NOTES
FROM THE UNDERGROUND

I jog away from Marianne's, trying to outrun the image of my friend on top of my girlfriend. Kind of girlfriend, but close enough.

Cutting through the King Soopers parking lot, I don't see Gobble there, and I'm glad. A little of his pharmaceutical magic sounds good right about now. I have it planned out. Get home, get Ray's gun, and then take my dad's car and drive it downtown to go do the deal. Then the suicide note. I'll lay low until Halloween night, when I can steal away Morgue's money.

I race by the security guard, up the hill, and around the corner. I see the moving van in front of Inga's. I hadn't talked to her in a couple of weeks, not since I introduced her to Ray. And of course now, I'm pretty sure Inga liked him more than me. Like Inga was an older, cooler version of Marianne.

When I see the vans and men carrying out Inga's stuff, I freak. I grab one, a toothless guy with a ponytail and way too much Old Spice spicing him up.

"What happened to Inga? What's going on?"

He shrugs. "No idea. They paid us to move her stuff out. Old woman like that, though, well, you know. She probably passed. You know her?"

I can't swallow. I have a pig in my throat, a nasty pig who hates the world and everything in it. Of course Inga would die. Of course, her friends or family would hire movers. "I have to know what happened to her," I say. "I have to know, dammit."

Ponytail guy shrugs. "Sorry, man. Me and the guys don't know a thing. But we can probably get you in touch with who hired us. If we got their permission."

She never married. She never had children. Probably friends are taking care of her things. I give Ponytail Old Spice my cell phone number, but I doubt I'm going to get a call. Really, I don't need one. Inga was ancient and too good for this world anyway.

My dad is in the kitchen, making a dinner I'm going to have to choke down as I pretend everything is okay. Hot dogs and macaroni and cheese. With salad and broccoli because vegetables are important.

I eat the food like I'm swallowing pills. I drink lots of water as my dad searches my face for clues. Why is there blood in the guest bedroom? Why is my bedroom now furnished like an Alcatraz holding cell? Why does the school counselor keep calling them?

We eat at the kitchen table, a little nook with a view of the movers eviscerating Inga's house.

My dad makes a comment, wondering what happened to Inga. Then he gets quiet and asks if I'm all right.

Me? I put on a happy face.

Sure, Dad, sorry I didn't tell you about my room. Gee, I'll have to put up posters of kitties and puppies right away.

Sure, Dad, a friend spent the night. He cut his hand. We bandaged it, but I guess we didn't do a good enough job. He bled on the sheet, but he's a white guy, so it's okay.

Sure, Dad, things are going better.

Sure, Dad, I gotta go. I have a ton of homework to do tonight. Thanks for doing the dishes. I gotta check in the basement for something first, but then it's up to my room. Gee, school is hard.

Sure, Dad, everything is just super.

The gun is easy to find in the guest room, under some extra blankets in the cabinet. I wait until my dad turns on the TV, loud enough to hide the sound of the garage door going up. I sneak past him with his car keys in my hand. I roll his car out of the garage without turning it on, and take off down the street. The moving van outside of Inga's is gone. Her house is empty. Dark. Lifeless.

At Sinastra, I pick up the drugs from K-Zee. It's easy to ignore his cracker-this, cracker-that tirade. I do the drop, go back and get my money, and then sit in my dad's car on the busy street in the posh area downtown. The beautiful people walk by.

Another thousand dollar deal for me

I pull Ray's gun out of my coat pocket. Here I am holding this gun, and I don't feel very *Matrix* or *Goodfellas*. It's just a gun.

I look into the barrel. Darkness, blackness, death.

I'm a big, fat, stupid liar. I lied to the only person who ever mattered. Me. I put all of my eggs in the basket of one hen, and the hen chose another rooster. And that rooster hadn't even helped when I was getting beat up.

And my other good friend is gone. Dead. Her stuff all moved out and maybe at the Goodwill. I can look for Ray's atlas of ye olde Prussia and give it to him as a going away present.

I have all the reasons in the world to just pull the trigger. Except for two. Two little reasons.

Again, no note.

And what will happen to Ray if I take myself out?

I know, I know, Ray stuck a knife in my back. Et tu, Ray Ray? Actually, they think Caesar had said something to Brutus in Greek. There you go, I'm about to shoot myself and I know so much about nothing.

In all the suicide talk, you get the basics down. Always take suicidal people seriously. If someone starts giving their stuff away when they're depressed, that's a bad sign. And suicidal people generally have this maniacal to-do list before they off themselves. I only have two items left on my list. Write a note. Make sure Ray is set up so he won't go back to the streets.

Ray is getting his life together. Now he has a girlfriend to complete the picture. He just needs some cash to get through the next couple of years. Just a little money for him to live on.

That's item number two. The hard one.

Item number one?

I know deep down I'm not going to come up with the perfect suicide note. I have nothing original to say. I can't say that life is too hard, and I'm too much of a coward to see it through. Nothing dramatic about that. Nothing poetic. Just the sad, sad truth. But I know I'll have to come up with something, however lame.

It's a little past ten when I get home. Again my dad doesn't hear the garage door. He probably thinks I've been in my room the whole time.

We wave at each other. I go upstairs to my bare room to get on the Internet. I hit Craigslist and jot down some numbers for cars under a thousand bucks within walking distance. Thank God for the Internet because I find around six right away that would do the trick. I just need a car for two days.

Two days until Halloween. Two days until Morgue's big cash drop with enough money to send Ray to an Ivy League college. And Marianne can go with him.

Lying on my bed, every time I close my eyes, I see Marianne and Ray, fully clothed, making out. Every time. Or I see Inga's flirty smile.

Doctor, it hurts when I do this.

Don't do that.

I stop closing my eyes.

If there is ever a time to relapse, this is it. I can go over to Todd's house and get some weed. Or go downstairs and snatch a bottle of anything and guzzle that bad boy down.

Sure. Here's Jim in soul-crushing, suicidal despair. He knows what will take him away from all of this. Why doesn't he?

I just don't want to.

That's the thing about drugs, alcohol, any addiction I think. It's that want. I want to eat my weight in Taco Bell. I want to smoke meth until my heart bunnies out of my chest. I want to watch porn until my hand falls off. I want. I want. I want.

The secret is not wanting. How you get there, dang, man, if I knew the answer to that, I could get my own infomercial and me and Tony Robbins could hang out.

For some people, like me, the want is removed. I don't want to get loaded. I'm already loaded, thank you. Drunk on my own misery. Drunk on losing the girl. Coming down off Marianne.

That's the thing. I assumed we would hook up. I didn't talk to Ray about her because I thought it was a done deal. Of course she would go for me. I'm the hip, bleak, black-clothed hero.

I'm the Suicide King.

What is she? Some goody-two-shoes Jesus geek. Or that's who I thought she was.

Three in the morning, I give up trying to sleep. I give up even the thought of trying to continue like it's business as usual.

I have to talk to 1066. I just need her for five minutes, and then I can be done with Coyote Ridge High School forever.

But first, my parents.

I flip open my laptop. This is going to be as close to a suicide note as I'm going to get. An email to my own loving parents.

I'm feeling exhausted and mean, so I send it to my dad and CC my mom. My mind is blurry and sodden, like someone dipped my brain in rainwater, but still haven't squeezed the muddy water out. I start typing.

Dear Mom and Dad,

First of all, you can't blame yourselves about what I did to myself. You didn't want me to feel guilty about your divorce, so you guys can't feel guilty about what I had to do. I know, you guys did the best you could. I get that.

I'm not mentally ill. I'm not stupid. I have free will, and I'm freely choosing to do some seriously stupid things. I'm selfish, I know, but I had to do this. Dad, I asked all the questions I could, but I didn't get any answer that made sense. I don't think there are any answers. Not for me.

Inga Blute, she had answers, but now she's dead, like Grandpa. I don't see the point. If we all just die anyway, I don't see a point to any of this.

You won't be able to find me, so don't try. If things work out, maybe I'll get through this. If not, I love you both.

Love,

Me.

I cry and cry and cry until I hit the send button.

I'm not crying when I leave my house to walk the chilly neighborhood, waiting for the next day to begin.

CHAPTER THIRTY-FIVE

AND THE BATTLE OF HASTINGS

I check my cell phone. I have voicemail messages, texts, and emails. From Marianne, from Ray, from 1066. Soon I know I'll get a deluge of digital worry from my mom and dad. I don't read the messages, or listen to them, no way. I'm in too deep, and I don't want anyone to pull me out of the morass.

Maybe if someone had called about Inga, I would've checked my messages. Maybe.

Thursday morning, sitting in my first class, alone, no backpack, no sleep, no hope, I have this eerie feeling. You know those guys who shoot up their school? Like what happened at Columbine? Sitting there, I'm feeling what they felt.

Numb, but hateful. Forever lost in dark despair.

First person through the door, 1066 comes in carrying my backpack as well as her own. She nearly faints when she sees me.

She looks good. Has she lost weight? Or am I just looking at her with eyes about to die? I don't know.

No, her hair is different. Or something. She looks good.

Maybe her concern for me makes her so smoking hot. I love it when people love me.

"Jim, God, I should've stopped you. I should've…" her voice fades away.

I don't have much time. My dad will be coming to the school. My mom will be flying home. The cops will be all over this town, scouring it, looking for Jim Dillenger. Man on the run. The Suicide King.

"You look good, Ten," I say. Even though I'm on the lam, I feel calm. Or maybe it's just because I'm so tired. "Do you like it when I call you Ten?" I ask.

She shakes her head. "No. I understand about the Battle of Hastings, but when you call me that, it's like you think I must weigh a thousand pounds. I don't like it." She doesn't say it whiny or anything. Just matter of fact.

"So why didn't you tell me this before?" I ask.

She sits down and turns around, our normal position. Her turning around to talk to me. Like I'm more important than she is. That's a laugh. She's brilliant, she can sing like an angel and rattle the windows with her bass.

What can I do? Except bitch. Really well.

"The nickname wasn't a big deal," she says. "I knew you liked calling me it."

I get up and kneel down in front of her. Might as well change things while I can. "Look, Cathy," I say. "I need to know I can count on you. It's about Ray."

"Ray didn't know," the girl formerly known as 1066 says. "He feels terrible. I should've warned you about Marianne earlier. And I never should've told you about her and Sutter and those other guys. Not right then."

I hold up a hand. "No, we're beyond all that. Ray needs money to live on. I'm taking off."

I see her eyes fill with buckets of worry.

I want to re-assure her. "No, not what you think. I'm not going to blow myself away or anything. I'm just going to leave for a while. And I need to get Ray some money." More lies for Cathy to swallow. I'm hoping my newfound talent for dishonesty doesn't up and leave me. "Look, I have a trust coming due, and so I'm going to have a lot of cash. I want to give it to you, so you can give it to Ray. Will you do that for me?"

She nods.

"Give me your address…"

She does.

"I'll call you," I say.

"Don't, Jim. Whatever plan you have, don't do it. Remember what Mrs. Shapiro said? She said you had to choose. I don't think you're choosing the right thing, Jim. Please, it was going so well with our study group. Please, make a different choice."

Sure, I'm all about free will, but at that moment, it feels like I'm locked in. That I can't change things even if I want to.

I stand up.

"Are you going to take your backpack?" she asks.

Another choice. Yes or no.

"No. I want you to have it. It's my favorite thing in the world."

Wrong thing to say. Alarms are going off in her, I know. She stands up and hugs me. I can smell her, the old 1066 smell. Cheap body spray, but it smells so good, because it smells like her, like every day at school. Like my whole life.

"Please," she whispers.

I pull back and see tears in her eyes.

I have to get out of there. I gotta get going. I can't stay because those tears will pull me back into normal life and trick me out of what I need to do.

Out in the hallway, I'm on high alert. For Sutter, who still has it in for me, for any teacher looking to hunt me down, for Ray, who I want to avoid, for my dad, who would be up reading his email, or getting a call from my mom because she's in a different time zone. My email to them is the reddest of red flags. Even more than me giving 1066 my backpack.

Gotta avoid them all, and Marianne, who I bump right into. She is radiant with love. Only her love isn't for me.

CHAPTER THIRTY-SIX

SHATTERED FAIRY TALES
UNDER THE BRIDGE

"Jim, God, I'm so glad to see you," Marianne says.

I walk. As in away from her.

She chases after me, running to keep up.

"Jim, it's not fair. We weren't together. We only had that one kiss, which was a total mistake. We were just friends."

I'm out in the open on the baseball/football field. Not good. I have to find cover. The nearest place where I will have any privacy is the bridge. Might as well head on over there, until I can pick up a car from one of the guys on Craigslist.

I know she won't follow me. The first bell is about to ring. She's too much of a Marianne to be late for class.

She follows me. She's giving law-abiding Christian girls a bad name. Missing class, sleeping with a bunch of guys, betraying me.

"Jim, you're going to have to talk to me at some point," she says.

Wrong.

I'm going too fast, and she slows down. Good. Now she'll drift away. She doesn't.

She keeps following me all the way to the bridge. We talked in her hideout, and now I guess we'll talk in mine.

It's so comfortable there. Like Cathy's smell. This is where I had spent some of the best moments of my life. I haven't been there in weeks.

The ditch smell slams my nose with mossy stink. The chipped concrete battles the graffiti for space. Cigarette butts are either scattered on the ground, or snorkel up from the fine sand where my loser friends and I etched pictographs in the swirling grains.

Every so often a jogger might amble by, but we were off the main path. The world wanted to leave us alone, like we were wasted trolls under a lost bridge from some shattered fairy tale.

"Welcome to the bridge," I say to my would-be girlfriend, my most-definite-betrayer. "I think you would fit down here better than you'd think."

She takes the jab like a trooper. Doesn't even pause to let it impact her. Until later, I'm hoping.

"Jim, I'm sorry. I messed up. I knew you liked me, but I didn't, couldn't…" she pauses, trying to catch her breath or think of something to say. "The way you were, if I would've told you I didn't like you like that, I was worried you would do something."

Somehow, sitting in my old haunt, I feel like I'm in control. Like I'm powerful or something. "Sutter warned me about you. He said you would break my heart."

Her face falls away, her whole head drops. "I keep messing up. I keep making mistakes." When she raises her eyes, it's like she's channeling some mythic goddess of anger. "You don't know a thing about me. No one knows how it is. How my parents are."

"So that means it's okay to go around banging every guy you meet? Sutter's friends? Ray?"

"I didn't have sex with them. I'm still a virgin!" She yells it at me. Tears course down her cheeks.

"Good for you. Your parents must be so proud. I'm wondering where your purity ring is. Or did it accidentally slip off?"

"Stop!" Marianne yells it. "You have no right to talk to me like that. I told you how I feel sometimes. Like I'm drowning. I'd forget about it, with those boys, but they wanted to get too close, and I had to run. Had to."

"Like you didn't have a choice. Please. You chose to be a slut. End of story."

She stoops down, picks up a rock, and throws it at me. I bat it away. Hurts my wrist, but I hardly feel it. I was used to getting stoned underneath the bridge, but not literally.

"At least I wasn't all suicidal. At least I tried to keep my drowning hidden and didn't parade my pain around." She apes me too well. "Look at me, I'm Jim Dillenger, and life is so hard. I want to die, and I can't find anyone to save me."

Ouch. I have to turn away so she can't see me wince. I turn back because I have to know. "Did you ever like me? Did you ever want to be with me?"

Marianne has her arms around herself, like she's trying to hold some kind of terrible beast inside of her. Then she hits me with it. "Yeah, I did, but you made it too hard to like you."

Her words sting. I prefer the thrown stones, but I have my answer now. I can go. Too bad I can't move.

She moves in for the kill. "You don't get to be suicidal without consequences. You wanted me to like you, but in the end, you chose your suicide over me, whether you wanted to or not. You're a selfish asshole, and why would I want to be with someone like that? At least Sutter and those boys wanted to live. And they liked me. You just liked me because you thought I couldn't help but fall in love with you and your angst."

My jaws clench, my eyes burn, my head throbs. I had assumed so many things. I had us married with kids after just one kiss.

"What about Ray?" I ask. "Are you going to do this to him?"

She opens her mouth, but I know that she doesn't know. She is too far gone. Weird, I thought only my little bridge crew had these dramatic, chaotic lives. I never once thought that Marianne would be so damaged.

I know I don't have much time. Once the APB is put out on the Suicide King, everyone and their mother will be looking for me. They'll check the bridge sooner or later.

I hope there isn't an Amber Alert on me. I'm seventeen. Maybe a milk carton, but not an Amber Alert. How embarrassing.

Gotta wrap things up with Marianne before I bolt. "So all your Christian-let's-save-the-world crap is just that, complete, unadulterated crap." I falsetto my voice and get prim just to drive it home. "'Life is a gift, but it's only a gift if you give it away.'"

She starts crying. *Always leave 'em in tears, Jim. You dog.*

I walk past her.

She grabs a hold of me, and I think we're going to fall into some mad, angry kiss. Like in the movies.

Instead she lashes out at me. "Don't you dare say that to me. Don't you dare throw that back in my face."

I snap back at her like a pit bull. "Why not? It's a lie. Keep lying to yourself, Marianne. And keep lying to Ray for all I care. You deserve each other."

This time she doesn't follow me.

CHAPTER THIRTY-SEVEN

HOURS DEAD

When you miss school, like when you're sick or too hungover, time gets all funky. At school, it takes forever to get to eleven a.m. But when you're not in school, time skips eleven a.m. completely, and suddenly it's noon, then three.

Just like that. Time speeds away from me.

I pay for my junky Craigslist car in cash. Twelve hundred dollars.

I pay for my motel room off of Federal in cash. Thirty-two dollars a night.

Then I wait for Halloween night, paying in blood, sweat, and tears. Apologies to Winston Churchill.

The room is narrow. Maybe that's why I can smell the bathroom from the bed. I don't want to think about what funk is on the bedspread, so I take it, fold it up, and throw it on the floor. Touching the bedspread makes me want to wash my hands. Cracked, yellow tiles around the sink give me hillbilly grins. Both the toilet and the bathroom have perma-stain. Back on the bed, the sheets are toilet-paper thin. Chains strap down the TV to the pitiful dresser.

I watch a whole lot of nothing on the TV, but I'm careful to avoid any sort of local news. I keep my cell phone off. I try to keep my mind switched off.

I have to turn on my cell phone to check messages, to see if K-Zee is calling me. Before my big Halloween heist, I want to make sure my standing in the Denver gangster community is impeccable.

My head keeps going on all by itself. All night long. All day Friday. I want to hear from Inga's moving team. I don't.

Suddenly it's October 31. Halloween night. Suddenly. Just like being sick from school, only I'm sick from life.

Before I head out, I check my phone one more time, and I have a dozen new messages. From Todd. From Sylvia. Even two from Annie. I recognize the numbers.

My battery is low, but I risk it and listen to the messages. The theme is the same. Todd is going to do it. Todd is going to blow his head off. Todd is going to usurp the Suicide King.

And he wants to talk to me before he does it.

I exhale hard, turn all Martin Sheen in *Apocalypse Now*. I pace, I rant, I have heart attacks and lean on the bed.

I can't go. Everyone is looking for me. I can't go. No way. Never. Someone recognizes me, gets the license plate of my Craigslist car (a bad-ass 1990 Geo Metro – rusty bad red, uh huh, uh huh, but so right), and suddenly nowhere is safe.

I have a date with millions of dollars. I can't miss it.

Todd isn't worth it. No one is worth it.

Do I go?

Yes.

CHAPTER THIRTY-EIGHT

IN A STUPID SORT OF HEART OF DARKNESS

Ray hadn't been specific about when the money would be there. He thought it would start coming in around six p.m., but wouldn't start overflowing until midnight. I have some time, but not much. It's ten o'clock. No more trick-or-treaters. Pumpkin corpses from the smashers scatter some of the back streets I take. A few houses still gleam with Halloween lights, but most are dark. Fake monsters switched off are so pathetic.

I drive by the rat terrier and his construction worker owner, and the afternoon of the barking dogs seems to be part of someone else's life.

I'm at a stoplight, and who do I see?

Brad Sutter. Alone. Shuffling through the dark.

I know I shouldn't do it, shouldn't draw attention to myself, but I can't help it.

I roll down the window. "Hey, Sutter!" I yell.

He looks up.

I take Ray's gun from my coat pocket, and I push it to my temple. "I'm almost there, you psycho bastard!"

I see his face wash away into pale white.

"You were right about Marianne!" I yell. "Maybe you'll be able to collect on your money. If things don't go well tonight, it's suicide! I killed myself, only I got someone else to do it. So screw you, Sutter. We'll see what they can prove, and if you can collect."

I screech away, adrenaline making me dizzy, putting some life back into me after so many hours being dead in the graveyard motel room.

I'm still buzzed on adrenaline when I pull into Todd's driveway.

Then it hits me. This could be a trap.

I can picture one possible scenario. Todd, Annie, Sylvia, all call me to flush me out into the open. The minute I walk through the door, that's when the cops and social workers jump me. My parents would be standing on the sidelines, weeping.

I take the gun with me. They won't take me alive. I won't kill anyone who doesn't deserve it. Only myself.

I throw open the door to his house like an outlaw pushing through the batwings at the local saloon, Old West nasty and cowboy hardcore.

Pot smoke and spilled beer greet my nose. My crew are all worried, pacing around on the slimy carpet infested with the debris of a thousand parties.

Sylvia and Annie are wringing their hands. "Todd is downstairs. He has a gun."

"So do I." I pull my piece. Piece, who am I kidding? It's a gun. It's this idiotic piece of metal that men use instead of their penises. It means nothing. It's death on earth, but it still means nothing.

I start down the steps. Like the chick in *The Silence of the Lambs*. Into the belly of the beast.

"Todd, it's me," I say.

No trap. I should've known Todd wouldn't narc me out even if they came on hands and knees begging.

His basement is unfinished, hung with sheets and tarps, making ghostly half-rooms. The carpet is just remnants thrown on top of smooth concrete. His bed just a mattress on the floor in the back. Next to it lumbers a desk, straining to hold up a monstrous computer monitor and a desktop computer from the 1950s.

I move through the sheets, wondering if Todd is waiting to kill me. Not sure why I feel like that. Maybe a gun in your hand dictates the drama.

The truth turns out to be far more simple. And stupid.

Todd is in the back of the basement, on his bed, stoned out of his gourd.

On his lap is a sawed-off shotgun. The only light is from this tiny little lamp with a stained shade. Everything else is shadow and spiders.

He looks up at me. "JD, you came," he says in this sigh-y little voice.

"What are you doing, Todd?" I ask.

He pats the shotgun. "Doing what you talk about doing, JD," he says.

Holy God. Annie was right. I don't know what to say.

"Tell me why I shouldn't do it, Jim," he says.

"You should," I say. "And I want to watch." I sit down in his stained desk chair. I get out my phone and switch it on to video camera mode. "I want the video of it."

He's looking at me, horror spilling across his face. "JD, come on. You gotta help me."

I laugh. "Why? Life isn't worth living. If you want to be the big shot and blow your head off, I want to witness such a tragedy of errors."

It's déjà vu. I had said something similar when Ed, Fred, and Chad were going to date rape Sylvia. Only it wasn't date rape, just rape rape.

Now, it's just the same. Part of me is sickened that even stone-cold sober, I can still be such a heartless bastard. "Put the shotgun under your chin, then pull the trigger. Easy. I'll post the video on YouTube. You'll be famous."

I watch him put the shotgun under his chin, but his eyes are wide. The fear is eating through the drugs in his system, and he starts shaking.

"You're serious," he says.

"Yeah, I am," I say. "Ringside seat to a real-life suicide. Pinch me, I'm dreaming."

He lets the shotgun fall to the mattress. "No, not serious about me. About you. You don't care anymore, do you?"

I look into his dazed eyes, and for a minute, I want to shoot him myself. Too much truth is leaking out of his eyes.

"Jim, let's go back to being friends," he says. "Life isn't so bad, maybe."

I switch off my phone. He's not going to do it. It's just the cry-for-help suicide. He might as well have tried to eat all of Sylvia's birth control pills.

"Life isn't so bad?" I hiss. "Then why are we here?"

Todd's eyes fill with tears. "I can't get clean," he whispers. "You did it. I figured I could too, but I can't." He pushes the shotgun away. "It's not even loaded."

"Wuss." I walk away, through the sheets, up the stairs, and back into the living room where the bridge crew is anxiously waiting.

"Call the cops," I say to them, "and throw the bastard in detox."

I hit the door, get in my car, and drive away.

It doesn't matter. Todd doesn't matter.

Nothing matters except stealing Morgue's money.

CHAPTER THIRTY-NINE

OF AN EPILEPTIC HEIST MOVIE

Am I suicidal driving over to rip off Morgue?

Yeah, but it's that blind suicide. Like the trip Ray had been on. It's a stupid, ignorant suicide. Killing yourself with dangerous moments of life, doing things you know are wrong in hopes someone will rip your heart out. Suicide by cop. Suicide by gangster. Suicide by someone else's hand.

I park on the street. Parties are everywhere. Costumed rich people caterwaul through the street, celebrating death and pretending to be scary. I creep through the festivities around to the alley behind the Sinastra. K-Zee isn't in his usual smoking spot by the dumpsters. Everything is cold and muted. The music of distant drums doesn't thrum as much as mutter.

The window is right there.

I climb up onto a dumpster, reach up to the filthy glass of the window, and I know it will be locked. It's not. It slides open quietly like it has been recently greased.

I only open it a little. On my tippy, tippy toes, I look in.

A security light behind me shines through the window, cutting a line of light through the darkness. On the desk are cash boxes, five or six.

Ray's gun is still in my pocket. I take it out and tuck it into the back of my pants. I open the window all the way, and then weasel onto the lip, huffing, the edges digging into my stomach. It's not pretty, but I get in, and not too loudly either.

Sweaty fear is eating holes in my stomach. My hands are flopping around like I'm inches away from an epileptic fit. It's far more *Trainspotting* than *Ocean's Eleven*.

Cash boxes.

Not locked. Stupid of them, but lucky for me.

I open up one of the boxes, just to check. Money. Lots and lots of one hundred dollar bills.

I figure I'll gather up a bunch, toss them out the window, then collect them up and make my getaway. Drop them off at Cathy Hastings' house, and then play Russian roulette with a semi-automatic pistol. Not much of a game.

I take one step.

The door slowly, slowly swings open.

I don't think about the gun. I don't think about running. I freeze, up to my elbows in a psychopath's cookie jar.

K-Zee steps in. "We've been doing the Halloween cash for years and years, cracker," K-Zee says in a low amused voice, not his usual ghetto patois. "A way to test the faithful, Morgue says. Well, we got one. Never thought it would be you. Now you're just dead white meat."

He motions for two guys to come in—the two who escorted me before.

I figure they won't think I'm armed, and with the gun, I might manage to shoot my way out.

They find the gun right away.

Just like that, I'm on my way to Morgue and his father's cleaver.

CHAPTER FORTY

IN MORGUE'S HEART OF DARKNESS

Same car ride. Same smell. Same handcuffs. Same blindfold, though I know I won't be around to show anyone where Morgue is after he's done using his cleaver.

Same elevator ride.

The doors open and it's the warehouse from before. The green shades of the lamps cast a sickly light across the disk sitting lonely in the dark. Classical music plays from speakers. The high ceilings devour the melodies. Not much music is left.

Morgue sits at the desk. Dead eyes and folded hands. Same black suit. No gloves this time.

"Hello, Mr. Dillenger," he says.

His thugs sit me down in the folding chair, but they don't leave. Not this time.

"I said, hello, Mr. Dillenger." Morgue is not happy he has to repeat himself.

This is my chance to play grown-up. I swore I wouldn't die a scared little boy on a cheap Wal-Mart folding chair. My email to my parents isn't really a suicide note. I need to make this my suicide note.

"Hello, Morgue," I say. I'm stewing in my own sweat. I still keep my voice normal. "So that's not your real name, right?"

"No, it's not," he says. He stands up and walks around his desk. The cleaver is in his right hand. In the dim light, I see both his hands are horribly scarred.

"So why did you choose a name like Morgue? Kind of obvious, don't you think?" Yeah, instead of making polite conversation, I'll bait the dragon.

The drug lord takes it all in stride. "I'm in the business of death. Like a morgue. What are drugs if not a way to die for a little while? Die to self. Die to the mind. What a waste, to squander one's minutes getting intoxicated, when death can strike us at any time. My drugs are death. And when people betray me, I visit a more literal death upon them."

I can't say anything more. He's feeling the edge of the cleaver with the pad of his thumb.

"Get the board," he says to his men. Then, as he appraises me with those dead eyes, he asks me, "Why aren't you begging for your life?"

I manage a weary laugh, and a part of me likes how weary it sounds. My eyes betray me though. They are full of weepy tears. "I'm the Suicide King."

One of the men returns with a sheet of plywood. The other man begins to take things off of Morgue's desk. The lamps go to the floor, the iPad is tucked away, the music is shut off.

The silence scares me, and I feel like I'm going to puke. All cool, until I start puking and crying.

"What am I going to do?" he asks.

When I talk, my voice cracks, tears stream down my cheeks, my nose starts running. I am hating myself. I am hating myself far more than I could hate anything, or anyone else. Even the man about to kill me.

"You're going to cut off my hands," I say. "Then you're going to cut off my feet, and you're going to throw me in the sewer."

"Not just throw you in there," he says. "I am going to chain you up, so you can watch the rats gnaw on you as you rot."

I find all of that funny somehow. Handcuffed, I can't wipe my nose, and it runs down my face. "I should've hung myself, huh? That's sounding better and better."

"When you came here tonight, did you come for the money or the suicide?"

"I didn't care." The truth. The absolute truth.

He motions for his men to take me.

They uncuff me and force my left hand down on the wood.

"It generally takes me one strike," he says.

"Thanks," I murmur. Like he's doing me a favor.

"What's good about life, Mr. Dillenger?" he asks. The same question Marianne asked me, in the classroom, when she wasn't sure I was serious about my suicide.

I cry and cry. Sob. And it's my whole life in that warehouse. A grand parade of minutes, the minutes I've lived. I can't talk, but I have my list. I know what's good about life.

The way girls smell.

Sunsets.

Late nights with friends.

The way parents look at you when they think you aren't looking.

Ray. Ray and his big change. Watching Ray reorder his life with so much grace and courage. What will happen to Ray? Will he go to college? How will things go with him and Marianne?

Marianne. I think about Marianne and how close we had come to having something. It would've been sweet if I hadn't been such a colossal mess. I want to see her again, so I can apologize for being so mean to her. She should've thrown more rocks at me. I deserved more than just one.

I think about Cathy Hastings, singing. Who knew she could sing like that? Who knew she had eyes that color?

Socrates said that death is just like sleep, and at that moment, I don't want to sleep, I want to stay awake. Like I'm four, and I don't want to go to bed.

My Tool song, why can't we sleep forever?

Because if we slept forever, we'd miss out on the few minutes of life we are given. And in the end, we are given only just a few.

Morgue swings his cleaver, and the pain crashes through me, chokes off my tears, makes me howl, twist and thrash. My own dear blood flows out across the plywood.

CHAPTER FORTY-ONE

LESS PIECE OF FLESH

Morgue doesn't cut off my whole hand. Just my pinky finger. Just that one finger.

He grabs me roughly under the chin. I choke and gasp.

He sticks his face into mine, and I smell his breath. It's awful. Poison. Still, I'm breathing, and his stink is worth every breath.

"Listen to me very closely, Jim Dillenger. Mercy in my business is lethal, and yet, I will show you mercy, you pitiful Suicide King with a rough gangster's name. You came for my money, and I will not let you have it. You came for a suicide, and I will not let you have it. You will live, but I have marked you. If you go to a hospital, if you go to the police, if you mention my name in vain, I will murder your family and friends and drown you in a sea of blood. Do you understand me?"

I can't do anything but look into those soulless eyes.

It's impossible. He's the Devil. He is misery on earth. And he is letting me go.

He strikes my wounded hand to get me to answer him.

"Yes," I sputter.

"You are reborn," he says. "You were killed in this place tonight, but a new man will walk away. I suggest you enjoy your new life, and leave death to those better suited for it."

I draw my wounded hand to my chest. Lucky I generally wear two shirts. I take my overshirt and wrap my hand, and they lead me away. Don't even blindfold me. I think they know I'm done with them.

The last thing I see is Morgue pick up my severed finger to look at it closely. I can't imagine what he's thinking. To tell you the truth, I don't want to know.

He chose his name well.

CHAPTER FORTY-TWO

PRAYERS

Alone, in my Craigslist car, I just sit with my wounded hand clutched to my chest and wonder. Wonder that I'm still alive.

My suicide attempt has been grand. I have gotten my money's worth, but now I have nowhere to go. Morgue is right. I'm a new man.

The king is dead.

I'm reborn. Long live the king.

I start up the car and drive. The pain in my pinky stump is making me nauseous, so I stop at a King Soopers and buy some extra strength ibuprofen and a bottle of water. Stitches would've been next on the agenda, but Morgue had said if I went to a hospital he'd murder everyone I'd ever known, so it was home remedies only for me. Back in the car, I take my medication and hope the ibuprofen is up to the task of dulling the pain. Part of me is just glad I'm still alive, no matter how much it hurts. While waiting for the pain meds to kick in, I sit in front of the wheel, wondering what to do next.

If things were different, I'd drive to Marianne's house. But no way I can go there.

If things were different, I'd go see Todd. Strike two.

I know the hotel where Ray is staying. Do I go there? Strike three. You're out.

I drive to the church. Not sure why, but I need to feel that feeling I had when I was there with Cathy.

I expect it to be locked up as tight as a fortress because it's Halloween night after all. You lock churches at night, or else you'll wind up with vandals despoiling the place and screaming Satanic curses in the sacristy.

Still, I already had experienced one miracle that night. Might as well try for two.

I get one. Front doors are unlocked. I expect to see the priest praying somewhere, or presiding at some kind of anti-Halloween Catholic ceremony, but the church seems empty. I cross the hallway and find the courtyard. Dim lights glow on the face of the statue of Jesus at Gethsemane. Fear and doubt play across his face. Those doors aren't locked either.

Inside the courtyard, I take in a deep breath. The air smells like snow and cold, but oddly, I'm warm, almost hot. The pain in my hand feels distant, thank God. I walk past the benches and the plants starting to fade like the flowers in Inga's front lawn.

Inga. I remember her theology of everyone. We are all Jesus.

"Thank you," I say to the statue. My voice is a whisper because you whisper in holy places. You just do.

"I've not prayed before. I mean, you know that because you know everything I guess. But maybe that's not your point."

I close my eyes so I don't cry. "No, that's not your point at all. People don't need a god that knows everything. Before you came along, we had buttloads of gods, and they didn't do much except give people a reason to beat the shit out of each other."

I smile because the statue and whatever impossible, unknowable thing it represents didn't care if I cussed or not. Curse words are just another form of baby talk to something like that.

"We don't need an all-powerful, omniscient god. We need someone like us. Someone who is hurt and confused by the world, who doesn't understand anything, but still believes life is good anyway. How else could you forgive the people who crucified you, even when you felt so lost and alone?" I've read enough literature and footnotes to get a pretty decent understanding of the Bible. Enough to say what Jesus said on the cross. "My God, my God, why have you forsaken me?"

I had chosen to be forsaken, and still I had been saved. Because Inga was right, I was a Jesus. Like all people are. Broken gods wandering around pretending to be human. Even the worst of us.

"Thank you," I whisper again.

My phone rings in the quiet. Scares the hell out of me. I had turned off the ringer, but suddenly it's ringing. Chalk that up to miracle number three.

At that moment, I'm pretty sure it's God calling me.

I swipe the screen to answer. "Hello?"

"James?"

Couldn't be, but it is.

"Hey, Inga."

Yeah, it's God calling me all right.

CHAPTER FORTY-THREE

STUPID THINGS TO SAY TO GOD

I don't want to spoil the special thing the courtyard has going, so I wave goodbye to the statue and walk through the church.

"Inga, what the hell? You should've called me. I figured you were dead."

She laughs. It sounds like music. "I was dead for a minute. It's very peaceful. But they brought me back. Some friends pried open my mind, and I'm in a nursing home. Believe me, I never wanted that to happen."

I'm getting in my car when I hear Schatzi's happy bark. "What does Schatzi think about the new place?"

"He's a dog, James. As you pointed out, a very simple creature. Of course, he loves it. New people to scratch his belly. That animal is shameless."

I sit behind the wheel for a minute, so glad she's alive.

"I do apologize, James. It all happened very quickly, and I figured you thought the worst had happened. Well, not the worst, but the inevitable."

"Yeah, the inevitable. I get what you said now, about life being precious when you can see the end coming. I get it. No more *Weltschmertz* for me, thanks, I'm driving. Life is too short."

"You'll come and see me, James, right?" she asks.

"You bet your grandma ass I will." I wince. I might still be breathing, but I still can say the stupidest things imaginable.

Inga laughs at me. Right she should. "Oh, James, I fear I might swoon. Please do visit me. Grandma ass and all."

We say goodbye, and I know I need to go home, but I can't yet. It's all going to change again, once I get home. That's okay, but I want to hold on to my night a little longer. I still have some stops to make.

CHAPTER FORTY-FOUR

TEARS CRIED IN BASEMENT PALACES

I park outside of Cathy Hastings' house. The girl formerly known as 1066.

Just a house in a normal neighborhood in a normal suburb with 7-Elevens and grocery stores and Costcos and streetlights. Normal and boring for most people. A grand adventure, full of life, for the man with new eyes. Kind of like Inga's quests for mail.

Snow starts to fall. Fat, happy snowflakes. Dizzy, I get out of the car, in only a t-shirt. The pain is better, but I lost a lot of blood. Could you bleed to death from cutting off your pinky? That would be ironic. I die when I don't want to. I bet that's how most people live.

The house is dark. Cathy's jack-o-lanterns no longer glow with flickering candlelight. I can smell the ghost of burned candles in the pumpkins though, that Halloween fall smell. Add that to the list of what's good about life.

I pick a window and embrace the cliché. I throw pebbles at the glass until a light comes on.

Cathy peers down at me.

"Jim?"

I wave. With my good hand.

"I'll come down."

She does, and I'm ushered in, and we sneak down into their basement. It's finished, nice, with lots of sofas and a big screen TV, even a bar with a little kitchen. A kick-ass basement, all around. Why didn't we study here? Why had I never been here before?

Her parents, mercifully, stay asleep.

She looks at me and the shirt around my left hand soaked with blood.

"Morgue," she whispers. Ray must have told her all about our mutual friend.

"Don't say his name," I say. "I never want to hear that name again."

"You're alive," she says.

I want to straighten up. I want to say, "Yeah, the Suicide King can never die by someone else's hand." I want to get all cool.

Instead, I start to cry.

She's in sweatpants and a big sweatshirt. Not exactly lingerie, and they don't flatter her. But she looks at me with soft, blue eyes. Blue eyes, like a day at an amusement park by the sea.

She takes me in her arms, and she holds me, awkwardly on the couch, and my hand is resting on her side, above her hip. I feel how big she is. A week ago, I would've been repulsed. Now, it's good for her to hold me. Her smell fills my head. The comfortable smell of every day at school.

I move my head back, to look at her, and I feel the pull.

I go to kiss her.

She brings up a hand. "Not like this," she says.

God, I can't get a break. But I'm too tired to get all pissy. "Like what?" I ask.

She leans back, and both of her hands are holding my good one. "I've had a crush on you for years, Jim. But tonight, with you like this, I don't want it to start this way." She looks down, caressing my hand. "It would be too easy for you to regret it tomorrow. And I've gone this far without getting my heart broken. I want to go a little longer."

"You're my only friend left, Cathy. Well, the only friend my age. Have I told you about Inga?"

She shakes her head.

I want to tell her everything, but I can't. Talking feels like moving cinderblocks.

In the quiet, she says the most amazing thing. "I have lots of friends. And not just Ray and Marianne and the band. Lots of other friends. You can hang out with us."

Lots of friends? 1066? The girl who spent every day at school alone? Ate alone, was alone in class, except for me. What had I missed?

She takes my silence for what it is. Disbelief.

"Most of my friends go to Mullen High School," she explains. "And I have friends from girl scouts and from church. Not that Doug guy, but other people. Cooler. There's a big group of us. Come and be friends with all of us."

"And you and me?" I ask.

"Let's just see how things go."

Truth be told, it makes me like her even more.

You know, I started this whole suicide thing knowing how my life would turn out, knowing exactly how every second of my life would be lived. Suddenly, there are possibilities laid at my feet I never would've even considered before.

"Ray made it seem easy," I say.

"Why's that?" she asks.

"Ray remembered not to forget. He woke up from his life and started a new one, and he didn't complain and whine and get all suicidal. But me, I wake up, I quit smoking dope, and suddenly I'm such a drama queen."

"Let's go see Ray," she says, "right now."

I give her a long, uncertain look.

"He didn't know about you and Marianne," she says gently. "And I'm worried he might not be as cool and under control as we think."

I nod.

Then she kisses me, on the lips, and she doesn't pull away. She doesn't leave me hanging like Marianne did. She nudges my lips open, and her tongue slips through, sensual, smoking hot, full of a passion I never would've thought could come from the shy girl who sat in front of me for years.

The kiss has me zinging out of my mind. It's soft, wet and wonderful, full of endless, NC-17 possibilities.

Breathless, she breaks it and gives me a shy smile. "You can't sneak a boy into your house without getting a little something, something," she says with a grin.

Amen to that, my sister.

CHAPTER FORTY-FIVE

ALIVE WITH SNOWFLAKES AND FRIENDS

In a short ceremony, Cathy places my beloved backpack in my arms. I smile at all the scribbles and memories. Another thing to be grateful for. We throw away my bloody shirt, and she gives me a fresh towel as a bandage.

On the way to Ray's hotel, Cathy tells me about the panic and mayhem my absence has caused.

I ask if Sutter cashed in on my almost-death and she smiles at me.

"Brad got expelled," she says.

"Excuse me?"

She smiles. "This is such a crappy car," Cathy says. "How much did you pay for it?"

"A buck three ninety-seven," I say. "Tell me about Sutter."

"I warned you about Marianne," Cathy says, obviously playing with me. She's just getting more and more comfortable. And that confidence shines through, making her so pretty.

How could that be? 1066, pretty?

"You never got our English class, did you?" she asks.

"Got what?" I ask back.

"*Siddhartha*, Herman Hesse, the whole story of Buddha."

"Yeah, prince and poor people and sick people. Whatever."

"Ray recorded the whole thing, where Sutter was telling you he was going to help you commit suicide. I guess Ray was doing a project for his Social Studies class, and I lent him my video camera. Ray showed the video of Sutter to Mr. Gelb, and they expelled him."

"No way." Maybe that's why Brad was walking alone on a Friday night. He was probably wondering what he was going to do now that he couldn't torment the good people of Coyote Ridge High School.

"But not before Gelb made Brad pay off everyone. They didn't know where you were, but it didn't matter. Brad's parents insisted on it. So I made a hundred dollars off you, Jim."

"You bet on me that I'd live?"

"Always," she says.

Snow is getting thicker, and we're sliding around, the windshield wipers thwacking across the window.

"What about *Siddhartha*?" I ask.

"It was you, Jim," she says. "*Siddhartha* was all about you."

I don't argue. If we can all be Jesus, only makes sense we can all be Buddha as well.

The hotel where Ray is staying is right off the freeway. One of those places you can pay by the week, only they should pay you to stay there. Rough guys stare me down and women in tight clothes and too much make-up ponder me. But my name is not John.

"I'll wait in the car," Cathy says. "I think you and Ray need to do this alone."

I clatter up to the third floor in a rickety elevator behind on its maintenance. I find Ray's room, inhale deeply, and knock.

Ray opens it, and invites me in. His face is shadowy. "Jim, sorry about Marianne. I swear. I didn't know."

"Yeah, I know you didn't," I say.

His eyes drop to my damaged hand. "You pay a visit to Morgue?" I nod.

He unravels the bandage on his left hand. He shows me where his pinky had been chopped off.

I then drop the towel, and the stump on my left pinky is still weeping blood.

"Let's clean it up," Ray says. "I did a little studying on this and a lot of times with amputations, the blood vessels retreat into the stump, so the bleeding isn't bad, but you got to watch for infection."

"Thank you, doctor," I say. I could see Ray as a doctor. I could see Ray doing anything he wanted. All things were possible because we were alive.

I tell him about Morgue, and the hoax of the Halloween money. We wash my hand, and the pain makes me want to drink down a liquor store, but I soldier through with more ibuprofen. We then cover the wound with antibiotic cream, and I use one of the hotel's hand towels as my third try at a bandage.

"When you talk to Marianne," I say, "tell her it's still true."

"What's true?" Ray asks.

"About life being a gift, but only if you give it away. You know, when I thought I was about to die, I wanted to see what was going to happen to you, Ray. I wanted to see if you were going to go to college and do this whole thing. I wanted to see how you and Marianne would turn out. The point is, I wasn't thinking about myself."

Ray turns shy. "Marianne, I don't know, man. It was just one of those things. I wouldn't bet on us, but she's cool."

"She is cool," I say. "And you know, her whole God stuff, I think it's the truth. I don't know if you'll hear me singing hymns any time soon, but I think she's right."

"You believe in God now?" he asks me.

I hold up my hand, "How else can you explain it? When the Devil shows you mercy, how can you not believe in God?"

"We still friends, King?" he asks.

"Always," I say. Just like how Cathy would bet on me. Always.

I say good night to Ray, and as I'm riding the elevator down, I think about *Siddhartha*. I was the prince, above the world, and suddenly I saw the sickness and the death and I was overwhelmed by it all. That bad Sunday night when I almost let my friends hurt my ex-girlfriend. My grandpa dying like that, my parents splitting up, all of it. It threw me, because in the drama, I should've been the hero, and everything should have worked out for me. When it didn't, I didn't want to play anymore. I had thought life wasn't worth the pain, but it's like what Inga had said—there is darkness in the world, but we'd be fools to ignore the light.

I drop Cathy off at her house.

"You going home?" she asks. "Your mom is back, and your parents are freaking out."

"Yeah, but I got one last stop," I say.

"Marianne's parents will kill her if you stop by," she says.

"Not Marianne," I say.

"Who?"

"A friend," I answer.

Once I know Cathy is safely inside her house, I drive off. Just like what Ray would do.

My last stop. Todd's house.

I don't have to worry about pissing off Todd's mom or his parents. No rocks aimed carefully at windows. I can ring the doorbell if the door is locked, but the door is never locked. I go right in.

The house seems empty, though his mom is probably home.

I make my way downstairs. Todd is still alive, passed out or just sleeping. The shotgun is still on his mattress.

I watch him sleep. My old, old friend. My friend who can't kick.

I reach down and shake him awake. He looks up at me.

"What the hell are you doing here?" he asks.

"I'm sorry, man, for what I did earlier. I relapsed into being an asshole again, and I'm sorry. I'm sorry for everything. I'm glad you're not dead."

He's just staring at me. I know that a part of him is still completely wasted.

"Let's talk tomorrow," I say. "I'm thinking a treatment center might be a good idea. Maybe for the both of us."

"But you got clean," he says. "You beat it."

I half-smile. "I quit getting high, but I didn't get clean. I'm going to need more help. I can feel it. Maybe medication. I have a friend on anti-depressants and they really help her. Maybe they can help us too."

"Okay," he says.

I stand up to leave.

"You're not going to kill yourself, are you, Jim?" he asks. "Something's way different about you."

"Yeah, Todd. Life is short. I'm going to live every minute I can."

We bump fists, and I take off. I lock the front door behind me.

The snow is still falling. Snowflakes tumble through my eyelashes like confetti at a party I never want to leave.

SUICIDE PREVENTION

The Center of Disease Control reports that teen suicide is the third leading cause of death in adolescents between the ages of 15-24 and the fourth cause for children between the ages of 10-14.

Some factors that lead to suicide or depression, feelings of hopelessness, anxiety and feelings of being trapped in a life they feel they can't handle. When the pressures of life seem too big, they look at suicide as a welcome relief for escape. Other factors are:

- Divorce of parents
- Violence in the home
- Bullying or rejection by friends or peers
- Failure to find friends or success at school
- Feelings of worthlessness
- Substance abuse
- Death of someone close to the teenager
- Coping with teen pregnancy
- The suicide of a friend

Teens may forecast their plans with warning signs:

- Talks of death and/or suicide (even jokingly)
- Makes plans to kill themselves
- Worries that nobody cares about them
- Dramatic changes in personality and behavior
- Withdrawal from friends/loved ones
- Shows signs of depression/listless
- Shows signs of substance abuse problems
- Begins to act recklessly and engages in risk-taking behavior

- Begins to give away sentimental possessions
- Spends time online with others/sites that glamorize suicide and/or suicidal pacts
- Spends too much time in their bedrooms
- Difficulty concentrating
- Changes in sleeping/eating/dressing patterns
- Considers running away
- Dramatic changes in appearance
- Complains regularly of feeling sick
- Wants to stay home from school frequently
- Writes poems/stories or draws pictures of death

What Can You Do?

One of the most effective teen suicide prevention techniques falls to the parents, friends, and relatives of the teenager. If a teen feels loved and appreciated, he or she is much less likely to fall victim to teen suicide.

1) Talk about it! Don't be silent. If you are worried about teen suicide, encourage your teen to talk to you about his or her feelings. Listen carefully, and try to understand. Avoid showing anger or dismissing problems as trivial. Don't be judgmental. Prevention is more likely if you get the issue out in the open.

2) Show love to your teenager! Your efforts at prevention are more likely to be successful when your teenager feels loved. Let them know that you are here to help, but don't start solving the problems yourself. At best you can only help to *facilitate* a solution.

3) Keep lethal weapons out of your home. Many teen suicides take place in the home. It is important that your teenager not have access to pills, knives, guns, ropes, or other deadly weapons. You want to make it as difficult as you can for your teen to carry out his suicidal plans.

4) Get professional help. You can call your family doctor for guidance and for a referral. Professionals are very good at helping teenagers to cope with their problems. Some teens prefer to talk about their feelings to someone who is not emotionally involved. Family counseling sessions can also help to show your suicidal teen that he or she is not alone.

5) Residential suicide prevention facilities. If you are worried that you can't watch your teenager all day every day, you might consider a residential facility. There are boarding schools and residential facilities that specialize in treating teen depression and focus on teen suicide prevention. These facilities offer around the clock care, counseling, and a special watch to prevent teens from committing suicide.

Information compiled and written by Donna Jantz, LPC. Taken from her Quick Companion Parent Guide: Begin Powerful Steps to a Happier Family in Minutes which is available online at http://donnajantzlpc.com/.

READER DISCUSSION QUESTIONS

1) Jim Dillenger, or JD, is the first-person narrator of his own brush with suicide. Do you think he's a reliable narrator? He speaks with certainty, but is he really that sure of himself?

2) Consider the ironic title, *Long Live the Suicide King*. What are other instances of irony in the story?

3) How does the writer use humor to deal with a dark subject? Is the humor ever too much or too disrespectful? Does this matter?

4) The character of JD could be considered spoiled and whiny. How does the author keep him sympathetic?

5) What is JD's relationship to God? Why can't he simply be an atheist?

6) Did you find yourself wanting to talk to JD about suicide? What would you say to him early in the book?

7) Many of the characters have dual natures, the good with the compromised. What are some examples and how do these dualities help JD solve his dilemma?

8) Why can't JD see the truth in Inga's statement about life being an adventure early in the book? Why does it take him so long to realize he wants to live?

9) Do you agree Jim is both Jesus and the Buddha? Why or why not?

10) Through the novel, JD asks people why they go on living. How would you answer this question?

Acknowledgements

On October 7, 1986 I came the closest I hopefully will ever come to committing suicide. If it hadn't been for my parents, I would've pulled the trigger. They loved me, and I loved them, and I didn't want to murder parts of them by killing me. It's why I'm alive today.

On that bad Tuesday, while I contemplated bleach, razor blades, and bullets, I found a note of encouragement from Jean Martin. She thought my writing was magical. Right then, however difficult or terrifying the journey, I knew I had a sacred duty to write fiction. It's why I write today.

This is the first book I wrote after attending my first Big Sur Writers Workshop. When I say attending, I really mean being reduced to ashes and rebuilt. Barry Eisler gave me some good tips on how to rebuild. It's why this book has a structure.

This is my first book that was fully critiqued, from first sentence to last. Thanks to one of my biggest fans, Jan Gurney, who believed in me when I was sure I was nothing to believe in. And thanks to Diane Dodge, who made me question every sentence. While she was a fan too, she knew I needed some red ink to rein me in. It's why this novel is less *The Brothers Karamozov* and more *Notes from Underground.*

JD's story wouldn't have seen the light of day if it hadn't been for Deb Courtney of Courtney Literary. She edited me, she had confidence in my abilities, and she adored me even though I cut off all my hair. She is the reason why this book is published.

Thanks to my new critique group, Mario Acevedo, Warren Hammond, Angie Hodapp, and Jeanne Stein for weathering the storms with me. Thanks to my new personal assistant, Emily Singer, for her digital skills and for breakfast. Thanks to Tamara Bryan Murphy and her medical expertise on severed pinky fingers.

Once again, Chris Devlin showed up right when I needed her and did all the right things, from line edits to discussion questions; she is a literary angel.

Once again, Steve Jankowksi photographed me and didn't laugh at me too much.

And once again, my wife Laura gave me her precious minutes. Ever enthusiastic, she supports me, as I continue to pursue this very real, very imperfect dream.

Lastly, for my readers. Thank you. Now, drink up, the buffet line is open, and this party, while it can be hard sometimes, is worth it.

Life is sweet.

About The Author

Aaron Michael Ritchey grew up dancing with the demons of despair, but around nineteen he got tired of demons stepping on his toes. So he's found other things to do like running triathlons, doing house exchanges across the globe with his two rockstar daughters and his movie star wife, and working a day job in medical technologies. He lives in Colorado and writes. A lot. It's far better than dancing with demons. Each year, the diabolical music gets a little quieter. A little quieter. *Long Live the Suicide King* is his second novel.

For more about Aaron Michael Ritchey, go to his website at www.aaronmritchey.com, friend him on Facebook, or follow him on twitter, @aaronmritchey.